"Miss Fairchild? Scott Blake. It Seems We Keep Missing Each Other."

"We've hardly been missing each other. You've been avoiding me. You left me no option other than arriving unannounced. I'll get right to my business, since I assume your time is valuable—I know mine is. We want your participation in our fund-raiser. It's all for charity. . . a very good one, too."

Katherine outlined the bachelors auction, then handed Scott a brochure summarizing the financial structure of the charity and the people involved.

Scott found himself intrigued by Katherine Fairchild. She might be a pampered, rich society woman, but the trappings of wealth could not hide her dedication and involvement where abused children were concerned. Her face became very animated and her eyes glowed with an unwavering dedication to her cause. He had to grudgingly admit to a growing admiration for her tenacity. That wasn't the only thing he admired—the woman also had great-looking legs. . . .

Dear Reader,

Happy New Year! And what a *fabulous* year it's going to be. First, due to *overwhelming* popular demand, we have another fun-filled lineup of *Man of the Month* books...starting with *Lyon's Cub* by Joan Hohl. In the future, look for *Man of the Month* stories by some of your favorite authors, including Diana Palmer, Ann Major, Annette Broadrick and Dixie Browning.

But Silhouette Desire is not only just *Man of the Month,* because each and every month we bring you six sensuous, scintillating, love stories by six terrific writers. In January, we have Jackie Merritt, Amanda Stevens (this is her long-awaited sequel to *Love is a Stranger* and it's called *Angels Don't Cry*), Kelly Jamison, Cathie Linz and Shawna Delacorte.

And in February we're presenting a special promotion just in time for Valentine's Day called *Mystery Mates.* Read and see how each Bachelorette opens the door to love and meets the Bachelor of her dreams. This promotion is so wonderful, we decided to give you six portraits of the heroes, so you can see each man up close and *very* personal.

Believe it or not, that's just what I have in store for you the first *two months* of 1993—there's so much more to come! So keep reading, enjoying and letting me know how you feel.

All the best,

Lucia Macro
Senior Editor

SHAWNA DELACORTE

THE BARGAIN BACHELOR

SILHOUETTE *Desire*®

Published by Silhouette Books New York

America's Publisher of Contemporary Romance

SILHOUETTE BOOKS
300 East 42nd St., New York, N.Y. 10017

THE BARGAIN BACHELOR

ISBN: 0-373-05759-8

First Silhouette Books printing January 1993

Printed in the U.S.A.

Books by Shawna Delacorte

Silhouette Desire

Sarah and the Stranger #730
The Bargain Bachelor #759

SHAWNA DELACORTE

lives in Southern California, where she has worked for several years in television production. She has always enjoyed writing, but it was not until she switched from non-fiction to fiction that she felt she had found a happy home.

An avid photographer who loves to travel, Shawna laughs as she says, "You should see me getting on a plane—my laptop computer hanging from one shoulder, my camera bag hanging from the other shoulder and my purse somewhere in between. Sometimes I actually have to hold my boarding pass with my teeth."

To Loretta
who often expressed great enthusiasm for my
writing. She tragically left us just a month before the
publication of my first book.

One

"Mr. Blake, that Miss Fairchild is in the outer office. She's phoned three times today and now she's here in person. I told her you couldn't see her without an appointment and she said she'd wait—no matter how long it took."

Scott Blake reluctantly tore his gaze away from the panoramic view of San Francisco Bay from his office window, high up in the Pyramid Building. He swiveled around in his large leather chair until he faced his secretary, Amelia Lambert. The expression on the prim older woman's face said she was unhappy with him—again.

"She's a very persistent woman, Mr. Blake. I truly believe she means to remain seated there until you've spoken with her."

A withering sigh of resignation escaped his lips as he picked up a letter from the corner of his large oak desk. The letterhead belonged to the Coalition for the Prevention of Child Abuse, a worthwhile charity well respected for its efficient operation. The letter was signed by Katherine Fairchild, the director of the fund-raising committee.

"Very well, Amelia." He loosened his tie, then his nimble fingers unfastened the top button of his shirt. He had never been able to get comfortable with the restrictive dress code of the boardroom. It had been five years since he had taken over the reins of Blake Construction following his father's untimely death from a massive coronary. And, at the age of thirty-four, Scott still disliked suits and ties.

He had worked summers on his father's construction crews while attending the University of California at Berkeley. His degree was in environmental sciences, not business, and he had planned a career in that area. As a child he had wanted to be a forest ranger. Upon graduation his father had talked him into remaining in the family business, allowing him to ramrod crews, even though he carried the title of vice president—working outdoors in the fresh air, rather than being confined in a stuffy office.

"Why couldn't she just ask for a donation? I'd be happy to write her a check. But this..." He waved the letter in the air. He swung his long legs around, swiveling the chair until the breathtaking view of the bay capped by the hills of Marin County once again came across his line of sight. "Let's get it over with. Send the officious Miss Fairchild in, but if she's still here after ten minutes, buzz me. And Amelia—" he turned his head toward her, flashed a mischievous grin and winked "—let her cool her heels out there for another fifteen minutes before you send her in."

He scanned her letter again. Even the ultrafeminine handwriting of her signature rankled him. Everyone knew the Fairchild name. Old-family money, sixth-generation San Francisco, the cream of society, on the boards of the most prestigious corporations, active in the arts, very influential in politics and major contributors to numerous charitable causes and civic projects.

There was always something in the newspaper about Katherine Fairchild, "Kat," as her friends called her. She was the only granddaughter of doting patriarch R.J. Fairchild and the youngest of Edward Fairchild's four children. Her mother had died when she was ten, the death cloaked in a veil of secrecy and the hint of a hushed-up suicide.

Women like Katherine irritated him. He had personal experience with them—pampered, phony, shallow, self-centered, vain. And now this. He stared at the letter, which had to do with a bachelor auction to raise money for the charity. She actually wanted him to stand up onstage wearing a tuxedo, posing in front of an audience and the media while members of the pampered rich bid money to buy an evening with him, as though he were a piece of merchandise. He did not like it, not one bit.

His thoughts were interrupted by the buzz of the intercom. Scott rose from his chair and prepared to greet his unwelcome visitor.

The news photos of Katherine Fairchild did not do her justice; she was far more beautiful in person than in any picture. Her finely sculpted features—he cynically wondered if any were the result of plastic surgery—were framed by lustrous midnight black hair, perfectly coiffed in swirls that were piled high on her head, with just a trace of coiled wisps along her cheeks. Her intelligent turquoise eyes were large, expressive and surrounded by the longest darkest lashes he had ever seen. Her makeup was perfect and her smile radiant.

Scott extended his hand as she approached his desk. "Miss Fairchild? Scott Blake. It's a pleasure to finally meet you." The smooth masculine voice resonated across the desk. "It seems we keep missing each other. What may I do for you?"

Their hands clasped as she returned his firm business handshake. A soft, sexy, low-throated feminine voice floated back at him. The substance of her words, however, was a far stretch from her tone. "It's 'Ms.,' not 'Miss,' and we've hardly been missing each other. You've been avoiding me. You didn't respond to my letter and have refused to take my last six phone calls. You left me no option other than arriving unannounced and insisting on meeting with you."

He released her hand as his face set in a hardened expression; his jaw clenched and his voice took on an edge of irritation. So—she was one of those pushy feminists, determined to prove that she was the better man rather than being content to be a woman. He had been called a chauvinist on more than one occasion and did not take exception to the intended insult.

"Won't you have a seat, *Ms*. Fairchild?" He took delight in noting that his added emphasis to the "Ms." seemed to aggravate her.

She studied him for a moment. He was tall, probably about six feet one inch, with long legs and broad shoulders. His deep tan was enhanced by his sandy blond hair with sun-bleached streaks. His silver eyes were alert, taking in everything. They held her gaze without looking away or seeming to be embarrassed. He was not the most handsome man she had ever seen, but he was certainly very close to the top of the list. The only flaw she could detect was a slight bump on his nose where it appeared to have been broken at one time. If she were the type to rate men, she would give him a nine out of a perfect ten.

"I'll get right to my business, since I assume your time is valuable—I know mine is." She noticed the almost minuscule narrowing of his eyes and a darkening of the color, from silver to more of a medium gray. There was no other indication of his irritation. "We want your participation in our charity fund-raiser the last Saturday in October. Your obligation would consist of putting together a date prize package, making yourself available at mutually agreed-upon times for publicity photos and interviews, attending the auction and, of course, going on the date with the lucky winner."

Scott leaned back in his chair, picked up a pencil from his desk and doodled on a pad of paper. "You really think some woman is going to dig into her purse and pull out hard cash to go with me to some unknown place? What do you do if no one bids on me?" A hint of a teasing smile tugged at the corners of his mouth. "Actually, *Ms.* Fairchild—"

"If the 'Ms.' bothers you that much, please feel free to call me 'Katherine.'"

He cocked his head as he coolly appraised her. "Or 'Kat'—isn't that what the newspapers say?"

Her voice was solicitous. "If that will make you happy, then please do."

"As I was saying, *Kat*—" he shot her a gleeful smirk "—isn't this closely akin to blatant sexism...even prostitution? Your wanting me to sell my wares to the highest bidder? Isn't this the embodiment of everything you feminists so vehemently oppose?" He continued doodling, the results of his efforts beginning to look suspiciously like a portrait of Katherine Fairchild.

She remained calm and unruffled, to Scott's barely concealed disappointment. "Not at all. We certainly don't expect or advocate that sex be part of your date package. I'm sure the women involved aren't expecting to...shall we say, 'sample your favors.' This is, after all, for charity—" a quick expression of undaunted determination crossed her face "—and a very good one, too." Katherine felt very strongly about the plight of abused children. It was probably the only real focus in her life.

She was very poised and quite unflappable. He watched her as she talked. Her long tapered legs were crossed, with the hem of her suit skirt resting just above her knee. It went without saying that her clothes were expensive and probably custom tailored, but she also wore them well. He had a feeling she would look good in anything. There was a sultriness about her, even though she made no attempt to behave in a provocative manner; she was strictly business. Her hands rested casually in her lap, her long lacquered nails made it obvious that she never did any physical work.

"As to your concerns that the ladies might feel they weren't getting their money's worth, let me assure you that none of them is being hurt financially. You see—" she allowed her radiant smile to cover her face "—they aren't really bidding their own money. The auction is more of a publicity and promotional event to kick off future fund-raising campaigns, rather than a fund-raiser in itself. The money being bid is money that's already been raised. Of course, the auction is open to the public, so that anyone who wants to make a contribution via a bid is welcome to do so."

The buzzing intercom intruded on their conversation. He quickly grabbed the phone and, without waiting for Amelia to say anything, spoke into the receiver. "Not now."

Scott returned his thoughts to the question he was about to ask before being interrupted. His confusion was evident. "Then who bids?"

"The bidders are primarily volunteers who have worked during the previous year raising funds for the charity. They are bidding the money they have already raised, some from individual donations, some from corporate donations."

"Who pays for the date? Is that considered my contribution to your charity?"

"It can be if you pay from your own pocket. If the money comes from your company, then you might choose to take it from your advertising or public-relations budget, since the name of Blake Construction will figure prominently in all publicity."

"So that's how one of these things works. What happens if I agree to this and then for some reason can't—" he allowed a mocking smirk "—or don't want to go on this date? At what point is my obligation to this project completed?"

"Fair-enough question. You provide the date package to the winner and she can then take someone else."

"What does the date package need to consist of? Are there any parameters?" He found himself becoming intrigued with the idea.

They talked several minutes longer about the specific applications of the money raised and the various services and programs the charity provided. She handed him a brochure outlining the financial structure of the charity, the people involved and the allocation of the money.

He also found himself becoming intrigued with Katherine Fairchild. She might be a pampered, rich society woman who had never done a real day's work in her life—and probably never would—but the trappings of wealth and social position could not hide her dedication and involvement where abused children were concerned. Her face became very animated and her eyes glowed with an unwavering dedication for her cause. He had to grudgingly admit to a growing admiration for her tenacity. Perhaps that was not the only thing he admired. Besides, she had great-looking legs.

"Let me think about this for a couple of days. I'll call you with my answer."

"That will be fine. Other than the specific date for the auction, everything else will take place at times convenient for your schedule. We'll try not to interfere too much with your business—" she blatantly looked him over, making no effort to hide the sparkle in her eyes or the slight curl at the corners of her mouth "—or your personal life."

Katherine stood and extended her hand toward Scott. "I hope you'll accept our invitation." She flashed her best smile as they shook hands. "I'm sure you'll find it interesting . . . you might even have a good time."

Scott dropped his pencil on the pad and quickly came out from behind his desk. Her handshake had been business-firm, yet warm and feminine. She smelled good, too—some tantalizing fragrance he could not identify. Probably one of those custom-made perfumes that are supposed to blend with your body chemistry. Another trapping of the pampered rich. He watched as she walked across his office and out the door.

"Amelia—" Scott leaned against the doorjamb "—what did you think of Ms. Fairchild?"

"She was businesslike. Persistent but polite."

One of the things he particularly liked about Amelia was her forthright manner. She had worked for his father for twenty-two years and Scott had insisted she stay on after his father had died. Amelia probably knew more about what was going on inside the company than anyone did; she had a phenomenal memory and a good head for figures. He also had a great deal of respect for her judgment.

Amelia continued. "I was surprised when she sat quietly for the entire fifteen minutes—didn't ask me for coffee, didn't fidget, didn't ask a bunch of questions about you, just sat quietly."

Scott cocked his head and raised both eyebrows. "Really? That surprises me, too. You'd think one of the privileged Fairchilds would demand immediate attention."

He furrowed his brow in a moment of concentration. "What do you think of this bachelor-auction thing? At first I was dead set against it. It seemed like a bunch of rich women who were bored with their daily club meetings. But now I don't know. After Kat, uh, Ms. Fairchild explained how it worked and what the money was used for, it didn't sound so bad." He fought back a grin that tried to play with the corners of his mouth while he visualized her legs as she sat across the desk from him, then his mental image moved up to her turquoise eyes. "I told her I'd give her my answer in a couple of days."

"I think you should do it, Mr. Blake. It's certainly for a worthy cause. Besides, you might have a good time."

He sighed. "Amelia, how many times have I asked you to call me Scott? Mr. Blake was my father." He sighed again, knowing his request would be ignored.

Katherine Fairchild unlocked the car door and slid in behind the wheel of her Mercedes. She had been trying to formulate her thoughts about Scott Blake as she walked from his office to the parking garage. He was arrogant and certainly had not bothered to hide any of his preconceived notions about her. He obviously considered her a pampered socialite who had nothing better to do than dabble in charity functions. The other thing about Scott Blake that caught her attention was the aura of sensual magnetism that surrounded him. She found him very attractive and very desirable.

She had encountered, on numerous other occasions, the same type of attitude he had projected. At first it bothered her that complete strangers decided what kind of person she was without ever having met her, but after several years in the spotlight, she had become accustomed to it. At the age of twenty-nine she had learned to be comfortable with herself and who she was. She chuckled as she wondered if she would still be as comfortable when she turned the big *three-O*. A fleeting thought brought up from deep inside caused her to momentarily furrow her brow, then she quickly dismissed the intruding memory.

It had not always been that way—growing up in the constant glare of publicity had been difficult for her as a child. Without really knowing her, the other kids had either disliked her because her family was rich and powerful, or pretended to like her so they could use her. As a result, she had become very isolated and very shy. However, all of that paled in comparison to what her mother had done to her. Even now, twenty years later, even though she had come to terms with it, the memory still occasionally intruded upon her life.

She cleared her head of the disturbing thoughts as she headed her car down California Street; she had a meeting at the Hyatt Regency in the Embarcadero Center. She had hoped to have enough time to grab a quick bite to eat before the meeting, but Scott had kept her waiting and now she was pressed for time. The idea that he had done it purposely tickled her consciousness. But she set the idea aside as the valet parking took her car and she hurried into the hotel.

"Liz, I'm so sorry to keep you waiting." Katherine set her attaché case on the table in the second-floor conference room as her practiced gaze quickly took in the others seated around the table. Her gracious smile included everyone as she acknowledged their presence. "Ladies and gentlemen, my apologies for my tardiness. Now—" she seated herself at the head of the table "—shall we get down to business?"

Elizabeth Torrance, executive director of the charity, returned Katherine's smile. "Don't worry about it. Jim just arrived moments before you."

Jim Dalton chuckled and good-naturedly added, "Whatever it is you want, you get my vote, Katherine. Thanks for removing the stigma from my late arrival."

Katherine laughed, too. "Jim, as much money and support as your corporation provides our cause during the course of the year, you can be as tardy as you like." She flashed him a dazzling smile. "And if you'd like to double your contribution next year, I'll let you be late twice as often."

"You'd better quit while you're ahead, Jim. You know you can't win with Katherine when it comes to fund-raising. She'll get your money one way or the other." Liz was a striking woman in her late forties who worked long hours making the monies raised stretch as far as possible to provide the maximum amount of help and services. She called the meeting to order and everyone got down to serious business—planning the next fund-raising campaign.

Katherine took control of the meeting. "I've just come from talking to our last bachelor holdout for October's auction, Scott Blake of Blake Construction. He's been ignoring our efforts to enlist his services. I explained the work our organization does and he seemed to be a little more receptive to the idea. I think he'll come around."

Liz brought the others up to date on the reasons they were so anxious to have Scott Blake participate in the auction. "He'll be a good one to have. There was a lot of good publicity surrounding him following the earthquake in October, 1989. The very next day he had a crew out inspecting every structure his company had built and scheduling repairs of any quake damage. Rumors circulated that he made repairs at no charge for senior citizens on a fixed income who didn't have quake insurance. When the press caught up with him at a construction site and asked about it, he refused comment, grabbed a hard hat, climbed a ladder and disappeared through the construction. Lots of people and companies gave lip service, but he actually did something, while shunning the publicity. That's the quality of person we want to have associated with our work."

The fragrance of Katherine's perfume stayed with Scott long after she had left his office. He had very mixed feelings about her. There were his preconceived notions about her type of woman, then there was the reality of meeting her. As much as he wanted the two avenues of thought to coincide, they refused to become one. He had a nagging feeling his preconceived notions were going to lose. He tore the top sheet from the pad of paper and started to crumple it, his intention being to throw it away. Instead, without fully understanding the motive behind his action, he placed the sketch of Katherine Fairchild in his desk drawer.

Scott quickly grabbed three file folders and shoved them into his attaché case. He had a meeting and was running late; he should not have wasted that fifteen minutes making her wait. Now he would not have time for lunch.

The meeting with the Colgrave Corporation had been called to discuss details of the construction of their newest shopping center in San Rafael, across the Golden Gate Bridge in Marin County. Blake Construction had already built four shopping centers for Colgrave, situated in various cities in the Bay area. This would be the fifth project. The two companies had a very good working relationship built on mutual trust and respect. Colgrave wanted quality, not corner cutting. That was the only way Scott would do business. His father had built the company based on integrity and a quality product. The firm had an excellent reputation and Scott refused to do anything that would compromise what his father had worked so hard to create.

"I hope I haven't kept you waiting, Brian." Scott extended his hand toward Brian Colgrave as he entered the room. "I was halfway to your office when I remembered we were meeting at the Hyatt Regency."

"No problem. I was involved in an all-morning seminar, so it made sense to conduct our business here as long as I was already paying for the conference room. We have coffee, tea and soft drinks. Could I get you something?"

"Nothing for me, thanks." Scott removed the folders from his case.

The two men discussed the details of the construction project. After half an hour they were joined by George Weddington, the architect for the project, and two other Colgrave employees. The meeting lasted two hours, and ended with everyone in agreement on how the project would proceed. Scott shook hands all around and hurried toward the door.

"Hold the car!" Scott shouted as the elevator stopped and the doors opened, then started to close again. Someone inside pushed the Door Open button as he ran the last few feet down the hall.

"Thanks for waiting." A tantalizingly familiar fragrance wafted across his nostrils as he pushed through the elevator door. Two turquoise eyes surrounded by long dark lashes sparkled at him and a radiant smile met his gaze when he turned toward the other occupant of the elevator.

"It was no trouble at all." Katherine Fairchild pushed the Door Close button. "Which floor?"

"Street level." He allowed his gaze to slowly travel over her, from the top of her perfectly coiffed hair to the bottoms of her high heels. She was taller than he had first realized—without her high heels and her hair piled high, she was probably five feet seven inches. She appeared every bit as calm and composed as she had been in his office.

He flashed a mischievous grin. "Really, *Ms.* Fairchild, I told you I'd call in a couple of days with my answer. You didn't need to track me down."

"When I really want something I don't stop until I have it."

A glint of something passed through her eyes as she returned an impish grin of her own. The look was a little unsettling; he was not quite sure exactly what it meant. The elevator stopped and the doors opened.

"Ah, here we are—street level," she announced.

His gaze followed her retreating form as she walked to the valet-parking window and handed the attendant her parking stub. No doubt about it; she had great-looking legs and a fluid walk that was difficult to ignore. He quickly followed her. His body brushed lightly against hers as he reached over her shoulder to hand the attendant his parking stub.

Without warning she spun around to face him. A note of hesitancy crept into her voice. "Are you busy for the next couple of hours?"

A slow grin spread across his face as he attempted to adopt a look of innocence, but the shimmer in his silver eyes gave him away. "Why *Ms*. Fairchild, what in the world do you have in mind? Are we telling valet parking to keep the cars for a while? Do I consider this a 'predate date,' an 'interview,' so to speak?"

Once again the unflappable Katherine Fairchild remained calm, seemingly impervious to his sexist taunts. "Where's your sense of adventure? You'll never know unless you get into your car and follow me."

She turned toward the drive as the attendant opened her car door. After sliding into the leather seat, she rolled down the window and leveled a cool look at Scott. "Well? Are you game?"

Two

Scott was not sure what had possessed him to agree to follow her, but there he was, trailing her silver Mercedes across the Oakland Bay Bridge. He had no idea where she was headed, or why.

Katherine's car came to a halt in front of an older building in a poor neighborhood of Oakland. Though worn, it was the only building on the block to have escaped the ugly defacement of graffiti. Scott pulled into the parking space behind her and cut his engine. Several tough-looking boys—boys... that was a laugh; some were as big as he was—leaned against the surrounding buildings, eyeing him and his car.

He cautiously slid out from behind the wheel and walked to the driver's side of her car. He leaned against the door, his gaze nervously flitting from one staunchly placed person to another. "Are you sure this is where you wanted to go?"

"This is exactly where I wanted to go." She stepped out of her car, seemingly without a care in the world. Her gaze darted from one doorway and alley entrance to another, taking in everyone who occupied the block. Her eyes finally lit on one particular young man, standing in the middle of an alley. "This is Scott Blake, he's a friend of mine." Her voice rang out loud and clear as she placed her hand on his shoulder.

Scott followed her gaze to the alley entrance. A boy named Billy sauntered toward them, his left thumb hooked in his pocket as his right hand expertly fingered the switchblade he held. He slowly appraised Scott while keeping his distance—all the while, Katherine's hand remained on Scott's shoulder. Finally Billy smiled and addressed his comments to Scott. "How ya doin', man? Any friend of Kat's is okay here."

Scott shot a questioning look at her as Katherine quickly whispered, "Not now." They walked into the building.

The inside of the building appeared neat and clean. Even though the furnishings were old and sparse, the atmosphere felt warm and open. Seated behind the desk in the front room was an attractive black woman in her late twenties. Cheryl Johnston looked up from her work when she heard someone enter.

"Kat. This is a surprise, I didn't expect you until tomorrow morning." A look of relief crossed her face. "I'm sure glad to see you."

Katherine's manner was immediately alert. "Is something wrong?" Her eyes searched the room, seeking anything that looked out of place.

"It's Jenny..."

"Jenny?" Scott watched as Katherine's eyes widened, a look of trepidation quickly covering her features. "What's happened? Is she okay?"

"Calm down. She's here and she's okay. It's just that she's been asking for you all day, just wandering around from room to room looking for you.'' Cheryl smiled. "You know how attached she is to you, from the moment Billy brought her through the door.''

Katherine's face softened as her fears quieted. She turned toward Scott, then back toward Cheryl. "Cheryl, this is Scott Blake—Scott, Cheryl Johnston. Cheryl runs our Oakland center.''

Scott held out his hand. "It's a pleasure to meet you, Cheryl.''

She returned his handshake from behind her desk as she smiled warmly. "Same here.'' Cheryl indicated the stacks of paperwork in front of her. "If you'll pardon me, I'm up to my, uh, posterior in alligators. I'd better get back to work before the boss catches me goofing off.'' She shot a quick grin toward Katherine.

"Hopefully we'll have you some help soon. We allocated the funds at today's meeting. Now it's just a matter of finding the right person. This isn't exactly a prime location. Lots of people are uneasy about coming into this neighborhood.''

A small voice floated through the room. "Kat! Kat!'' Little feet padded across the floor as an angelic golden-haired tyke of about three ran to her.

Katherine Fairchild kicked off her high heels, dropped to her knees and held open her arms to welcome the little girl. Her voice carried enthusiasm and love. "Jenny, my little precious.'' She drew the child quickly into her embrace and held her tightly as she rocked her back and forth. Then she placed a loving kiss on the child's cheek. "Have you been a good girl today?''

"Yes, Kat.''

The little girl snuggled in Katherine's arms, her small hand closing around the soft silk of Katherine's blouse, tugging and pulling at it in her excitement. One final tug was too much for the thread that held the top button; it broke and the button popped off, allowing the blouse to gape. Katherine seemed not to be aware of the missing button. Scott, however, could not help but notice the delightful fullness of creamy skin that disappeared into the delicate lace cup of her bra.

Katherine lifted the squirming little girl in her arms as she rose to her feet. She swung around so they were both facing Scott. "Jenny, this is Scott. He's a friend of mine. Can you say hello to him?"

He smiled at the little girl. "Hello, Jenny." He saw the wariness come into the child's eyes. She pulled as far away from him as she could, wrapped her arms tightly around Katherine's neck and turned her head away, burying her face in Katherine's shoulder. Scott was both surprised and confused.

Katherine continued to hold Jenny, rocking the child gently in her comforting embrace. Her voice was soft and soothing as she tried to allay Jenny's sudden anxiety. "It's okay, Jenny. Scott is my friend. He won't hurt you." The little girl's head remained buried, her face hidden from sight. "Won't you please say hello to Scott? I'm sure he'd like to see your pretty smile."

Jenny's blond curls bounced as she shook her head, keeping her face buried.

Katherine's voice continued to drift softly across the child's being. "Please, Jenny, would you say hello to Scott...for me?"

Slowly Jenny raised her head and tentatively glanced around at the man standing next to Katherine. Again Scott offered the child a warm smile and reached his hand out toward her.

But tears welled in her eyes and she started to cry. A startled Scott quickly withdrew his hand and stepped back. Katherine held the little girl tightly as she buried her face against Katherine's suit jacket, her tears soaking the fabric.

Scott watched as Katherine carried the crying child from the room. Turning toward Cheryl, he seated himself on the corner of her desk. "What happened? Why did she start to cry?"

Cheryl's voice was filled with compassion and frustration. "It's a very sad set of circumstances. The child's name is Jenny Hillerman. Her mother's current boyfriend, in a long string of many, beat Jenny. Her mother did nothing to stop it." Cheryl's tone of voice clearly displayed her disgust. "Didn't want to take a chance on doing anything that might cost her the service of her current superstud."

She noted Scott's quick expression of surprise at her choice of words. "These are the streets, Scott. That was the cleaned-up version for your benefit. There's no room here for the polite words used by civilized people."

"How did you get her, or rather how did Billy get her?"

"He found her about six one morning. She was sitting in front of the apartment building where she lived—cold, bruised and huddled in the doorway. It didn't take long for Billy to determine that the mother and boyfriend had skipped out, abandoning Jenny. He brought her here. She's still a little wary of men, but she's coming out of it. Fortunately her mother had only been with the current boyfriend for a couple of months, so there wasn't a long history of physical abuse to try to overcome."

Scott liked Cheryl. She appeared to have things well in hand and, as he had observed of Katherine Fairchild, seemed to be truly dedicated to the work of the charity. "Are you here full-time—I mean, as an employee, rather than a volunteer?"

"That's me. File clerk, receptionist, chief bottle washer and a master's degree in psychology. It was Kat's idea to hire someone with a degree in child psychology rather than the normal situation of someone with a degree in sociology, social services or business administration. She felt that even if these kids are here only for a few weeks, it's to their advantage to start some type of psychological counseling as soon as they arrive.

"We try to be more than just a temporary facility for these kids until they are returned to their own homes or placed in foster homes. The really young ones, like Jenny, have a good chance of coming through things without permanent scars if we can get them help right away. The length of time they've been exposed to the abuse is shorter, therefore the amount of damage we have to undo is much less. In Jenny's case it's much less because it wasn't her mother who did the beating, and as I said, it was a very recent situation with the mother's current boyfriend.

"We have to let these kids know that someone cares about them. Kat is adamant on the subject. These kids need to know that they're not alone and that what has happened to them is not their fault." Cheryl glanced in the direction that Katherine had taken the little girl. "Jenny is going to be just fine. She couldn't ask for anyone better to take care of her than Kat."

A thought was formulating in the back of Scott's mind, something that would never have occurred to him had he not been at the center. "Kat said something about getting you some help. Exactly what type of help are you looking for?"

"I'll take any type of help I can get. Mostly I need someone who's organized, good with paperwork and people and able to deal with pressure and stress. Any time you do something connected with any government agency, there's twice the paperwork. I guess what I really need is someone who can function as my administrative assistant. That's a very fancy title that means doing a little bit of everything and not having anyone except me appreciate it. I need someone who can take part of this load—" she indicated the stacks of file folders on her desk "—off me and let me spend more time working with the kids." She cocked her head and gave Scott a questioning look. "Do you have someone in mind?"

Scott smiled at Cheryl and gave her a quick wink as he stood up. "I just might."

"I think we're okay for now." Katherine's voice came from the rear door as she entered the room. "Jenny's asleep." She turned her attention to Scott. "I'm sorry about the interruption. She's still uncertain about her surroundings and wary of new people. I thought she might take to you if she saw you with me. . . ." Her voice trailed off. "I guess it's just going to take more time."

Her expression brightened. "Come, let me give you a tour." She grabbed his hand and pulled him across the room. "I want you to see what our work is all about."

Even after she had released his hand the tingling warmth of her touch lingered. For half an hour she showed him around the building and explained how this particular center functioned between the reality and needs of the people in the community and the bureaucracy of government agencies and the courts. The center was licensed to house up to ten children at a time. It was only supposed to be a temporary place for them, but some were at the center for many months before their disposition was settled. There were six employees in addition to Cheryl.

"How does Billy fit into this? Cheryl said he was the one who brought Jenny in here."

"It's Billy Sanchez's neighborhood. He runs things down here. I first met him four years ago. This center had been open for three months and, like every other building in the neighborhood, was subject to constant vandalism. One day a tough, defiant thirteen-year-old street kid burst through the front door pulling a dirty bedraggled little eight-year-old girl behind him. He looked around and demanded to know who was in charge. Taking a deep breath and trying not to show my uneasiness, I told him I was.

"He looked me over, jerked his head toward the front door and asked if the fancy wheels out front belonged to me. I told him they did. He just sneered, told me I obviously couldn't know anything about anything and started to walk away. The little girl he had in tow looked so frightened, I just couldn't let him walk out with her—not until I knew what was going on. I reached out and grabbed his arm, pulling him to a halt."

"It would seem to me, *Ms.* Fairchild, that you had just done a very foolish thing."

"That was the conclusion I came to when he wheeled around and glared pure venom at me. He jerked his arm out of my grasp and told me never to touch him again if I knew what was good for me. I held his gaze, determined not to look away or flinch. After what seemed like an eternity he began to soften.

"The little girl with him was his sister. His story was my first experience in dealing directly with the horror of the everyday lives of the people we're trying to help. Up until then I had only seen the fund-raising side—using my contacts to solicit donations, attending meetings, organizing events—" she paused long enough to shoot him a knowing look "—all the things you assumed to be my sole function in life."

Katherine watched the embarrassment flicker through his eyes and a hint of color come to his cheeks. "You see, Scott, it's been a constant uphill battle to combat people's preconceived notions about me. It seems that everyone wants to believe the worst. I suppose it's human nature, but that doesn't make it any easier to live with."

He felt a twinge of embarrassment. He wanted to say something in defense of his attitude and thoughts, but there was nothing to say. She had nailed him but good. He caught the fleeting look of anguish in her eyes before she continued.

"Billy's father had deserted the family shortly after his sister was born. His mother became a junkie. As soon as she was hooked, her pusher turned her on to prostitution. He added her to his stable of women, all hooked on junk. Billy dropped out of school in seventh grade and spent most of his time on the streets, picking up odd jobs where he could and stealing when necessary.

"His prime objective was to protect his sister. He had long since written off his mother. He came home one day and found his mother totally out of it and her 'customer' trying to rape his sister."

Scott flinched noticeably. "My God..."

"Being a man of action rather than words, Billy grabbed the first thing he could find, bashed the would-be attacker over the head, grabbed his sister and took off. He wasn't sure where to go—he could always find a place to sleep on the streets, but he knew his sister needed somewhere safe. There was no way he'd ever go to the authorities, so he screwed up his courage and came here.

"We gave her a hot meal, a bath, clean clothes and a warm bed. He came back the next day to see how she was. When he found out everything was okay, he gave us his stamp of approval. From that day forward, we haven't had any problems. Billy's boys watch over the center and carefully screen all strangers who come into the neighborhood."

"Yes, I noticed them giving me the serious once-over."

"That's why I immediately told them who you were. Otherwise, you probably wouldn't have a car when you tried to leave."

Scott smiled. "Thanks for the help. I appreciate it and so does my insurance company." His manner turned serious. "What happened with Billy's sister?"

"We found a nice foster home for her. At first the courts gave us a lot of trouble—the child needing to be returned to the care of the mother—" he saw the anger in Katherine's eyes as she continued "—without regard for the kind of atmosphere or the danger she'd be returned to. The problem was quickly, but tragically, resolved. The next month the mother died of an overdose. There being no known relatives other than Billy, the rest was routine."

"I must say, *Ms.* Fairchild—"

"Could you please drop the 'Ms.'? I feel that we're past that—don't you?"

Her smile dazzled him as he again saw the sparkle in her turquoise eyes. He held her gaze for a long moment, his pulse rate increasing ever so slightly. "Yes, I believe you're right."

Scott drove back across the Oakland Bay Bridge, his mind filled with the sights and words he had absorbed over the previous two hours. It had really been an eye-opening education. If Katherine Fairchild felt his participation in a bachelor auction would help the cause, then it would certainly be petty of him to refuse simply because it was inconvenient or made him feel awkward. He would call her first thing in the morning.

Deciding not to bother going back to his office, he drove through town and continued on across the Golden Gate Bridge to the Tiburon exit. Skirting the bay, he turned onto a winding side road and climbed the hill until he came to the circular drive.

The older house stood high on the hill overlooking the bay, Angel Island, Alcatraz, the towers of the Golden Gate, the skyline of San Francisco. Scott had always loved this view. He was glad his mother had decided to keep the house after his father had died. At first she had been afraid there would be too many memories for her to handle, but had finally realized they were mostly good ones, of warm and loving times—she did not want to lose them.

"Mom? Hello, is anyone home?" Receiving no answer, he wandered through the house toward the backyard.

Looking through the back screen door, he found Lynn
Blake working in her garden. He watched his mother for a
moment. For a woman fifty-six years old, she was remark-
ably youthful in appearance and possessed the energy of
someone at least fifteen years younger.

"You know, Mom—"

Lynn Blake's startled face looked up at the intrusion of
the male voice. "Scott! What a surprise."

"You're really much too vibrant a woman to spend your
time and energy just working in the yard. How would you
like something really worthwhile to do?"

"Uh-oh, what are you trying to get me involved in now?
You know how much I love my garden."

He noted the suspicious look in her eyes, and offered her
his most charming smile. "Why don't we go out to dinner—we haven't done that for quite a while."

"I see—'Welcome to my web,' said the spider to the
fly.'" Lynn Blake returned her son's smile as she gathered
her things and walked across the yard. "Give me a few
minutes to clean up and change clothes, then I'll be happy
to endure yet another of your many plans for getting me out
of the house more often."

"You're going to like this one. It's right up your alley,"
he replied with all the enthusiasm he could muster.

Scott wandered around the living room while waiting for
his mother. He carefully picked up framed photographs,
looked at them and set them down. He, too, had many
good memories of the house, memories of a happy childhood spent with loving parents: a father who was never too
busy to go out in the yard and play catch with a little boy,
even though he worked long hours building up his own
business; a mother who always had time to read him a
bedtime story, even though her days were taken up by her
job as a schoolteacher and her evenings spent taking care
of the house and her family.

His mind drifted to family camping trips in the mountains, which had instilled in him his love of nature and concern for the environment. His father had taught him how to identify plants and birds, how to recognize geologic formations and what they meant, how to hike a trail without making a negative impact on the wilderness. He thought of family weekend outings and what his mother had always referred to as 'our Sunday afternoon drive.' There was always something new—the zoo, the aquarium, a museum—always something to stimulate his curiosity.

A pang stabbed him as he thought about how ideal his childhood had been, especially compared with Billy's and his sister's, and little Jenny Hillerman's. He felt ashamed that he had ignored Katherine Fairchild's letter and phone calls without even bothering to find out what they were about. His thoughts were interrupted by his mother's return.

"I guess I'm ready." Lynn Blake gave her son a knowing smile. "I don't suppose you'd like to tell me what this is all about right now and get it over with before we eat, would you?"

"No, I don't suppose I would." He held the front door open for his mother as he tried to suppress a little grin.

Katherine Fairchild pulled her Mercedes into the long drive leading to the large house in Saint Francis Woods, the most exclusive section of San Francisco. It had been a couple of weeks since she had visited her grandfather. He had been confined to a wheelchair for almost five years and was not in the best of health. She did not like to go this long between visits, but the plans for the charity auction and the upcoming fund-raising campaign had kept her very busy. She also had not spent as much time at the Oakland center as she would have liked.

"Grandpa, how are you feeling?" Katherine knelt next to his wheelchair, giving him a big hug and kiss on the cheek. "You're looking good."

R.J. Fairchild gave his granddaughter a stern look. "Katherine, how many times do I need to tell you that 'grandpa' is not a proper term? The word you are looking for is 'grandfather.'"

She refused to be put off by his scolding and gruff attitude. From the time she was a little girl she had been able to wrap the formidable R.J. Fairchild around her finger. She gave him a knowing smile and another kiss on the cheek.

His gnarled old hand patted her hand as he gave her a loving look. "Don't you dare let anyone else hear you call me that. How can I maintain a position of respect when my own granddaughter... ?"

"Stop being an old fuddy-duddy. You can pull that stuff on other people but not on me. You know you like it when I call you Grandpa." She stood up and pushed his wheelchair into the garden room at the back of the house. "I met a very interesting man today, Grandpa."

The old man's attention immediately perked up. "Did you? Does this mean I might at long last hear the patter of little feet, be able to look at my great-grandchild before I die?"

"Stop being so dramatic," she teased. "You're a long way from dying and you have lots of great-grandchildren. All three of my brothers have provided you with great-grandchildren and Uncle Charlie's two sons have given you great-grandchildren. I'll bet you can't even remember the names of all your great-grandchildren."

"It's not the same, Katherine. You are the only girl. I have no daughters and you are my only granddaughter. You should be providing me with great-grandchildren."

"Really, Grandpa. It's almost the twenty-first century—get with the times. Women have a place in the world other than cleaning house and making babies." She poured them each a glass of wine from the bar cart and sat next to him. Everyone else found him irascible and intimidating. No one dared talk to him the way Katherine did. She dearly loved the old man and he clearly doted on her.

"I am too old to 'get with the times,' as you say. Now, tell me about this young man. What does he do and where did you meet him? I want to know all about his background. We can't have another situation like that—"

"Please, Grandpa." She cut him off before he could finish his sentence. She knew exactly what he was going to say... another situation like her impetuous and ill-fated marriage to Jeff during her sophomore year of college—a situation that had cost the family $250,000 and left her with deep scars of hurt and definite opinions where marriage was concerned. It had been yet another childhood legacy left to her by her mother. It had taken a long time for the wounds to heal, for her to rebuild her self-esteem and get on with her life. "All I said was that I had met an interesting man. I didn't say anything about a potential husband."

"Katherine—" he reached out and took her hand in his "—you're almost thirty years old. Don't you think it's time you married and started a family?"

A frown wrinkled her brow; a faraway haunted look passed briefly across her face. Even now an occasional memory from the past would try to reestablish itself. "I'm not looking for another husband. I've already had one, remember?" She offered him her best smile. "Now, can we drop the subject of husbands and marriage?"

He patted her hand and smiled. "All right. Now, tell me about this interesting man you met today."

Katherine remained with her grandfather for most of the evening. She told him about her latest activities with the charity: the bachelor auction and how Scott fit in, the newest crisis at the Oakland center and little Jenny Hillerman. "Grandpa, it just tears my heart out. You should have seen her when I tried to get her to say hello to Scott.'' She allowed a slight smile to turn the corners of her mouth. ''And you should have seen Scott when she started to cry.''

''And which one of them was responsible for that?'' he asked as he pointed to the missing button from her blouse.

She looked down, noticing for the first time the button was gone. ''Oh!'' She shot him a sly grin. ''If it had been Scott, I certainly wouldn't be telling you about it.''

It was late when Katherine left her grandfather's house. They had talked the entire time, just the two of them, and had enjoyed dinner together. Upon departing, she had promised not to wait so long until her next visit.

''Carruthers.'' R.J. Fairchild summoned his butler. ''Get Bob Templeton on the phone.'' A few minutes later, Carruthers brought him the portable phone.

''R.J., do you realize what time it is? Unless someone is in jail, attorneys aren't supposed to get calls at home at this time of night. Now, who's in jail?'' Bob's voice was demanding, clearly indicating his irritation at having to deal with a call at such a late hour.

''Cut the crap, Bob. First thing in the morning I want you to get me the book on Scott Blake of Blake Construction. I want to know everything there is to know about him, about his family and about his business. And Bob...this is highly confidential.''

Katherine pulled her Mercedes into the two-car garage of the ground level of her three-story house. Ignoring the small elevator, she climbed the stairs to the third floor—her private enclave shut off from the rest of the world. The entire third level consisted of her bedroom and bathroom, an office and a large deck with a breathtaking view of the bay and the green hills of Marin.

She quickly kicked off her high heels and shed her clothes, opting for a pair of jeans and a T-shirt. The thick carpeting felt good on her bare feet as she walked into the bathroom. She washed her face, removing all her makeup, then brushed out her long hair and pulled it back into a ponytail. Even though it was late she still had about two hours of paperwork to do before she could go to bed. Reluctantly she picked up her attaché case from where she had dropped it on her antique four-poster bed and carried it into her office.

Katherine may have been sitting at her desk, but she was not working. Her mind kept drifting to Scott Blake. Telling her grandfather that she had met an interesting man was an understatement of the greatest magnitude.

When she had told Scott she usually got what she set out after, she had been deadly serious. What she had not said out loud was that Scott was what she wanted, and not just for the charity auction, either. The moment she felt the warmth of his handshake, heard his smooth masculine voice and saw his dazzling smile, she knew he was something special. She was not exactly sure how—yet—but she would make him see the real Katherine Fairchild, not the woman whose name and picture constantly adorned the society pages and about whom he obviously had very definite preconceived notions.

Running into him at the Hyatt was a real stroke of luck—or perhaps it was fate. She could tell how impressed he was with the tour of the Oakland center and the work they did. There was no doubt in her mind that he would accept her invitation to participate in the auction. She allowed herself a few extra moments to speculate on what type of date package he would put together—perhaps an elegant dinner followed by the theater.

She shut her eyes and allowed an image of Scott Blake to dance across her closed eyelids. He was very tan, very blond and had about a thousand perfect white teeth that showed whenever he flashed his dazzling smile. Her breathing quickened ever so slightly as she recalled his silver eyes slowly looking her over in the elevator at the Hyatt. "You don't know it yet, Scott Blake, but you're mine—all mine."

Three

Scott opened the sliding glass door and stepped out onto the patio of his house, looking out over the bay. He, too, lived in Tiburon—right on the water, very close to the downtown village area and the yacht club where he kept his sailboat. The damp night breeze caused a slight shiver to rush across the surface of his skin. It had been an hour since he left his mother's house following dinner.

To his surprise, Lynn Blake had seemed fairly receptive to his suggestion about working at the Oakland center. She had promised to go with him the next afternoon to meet with Cheryl. He would call in the morning to set up the appointment.

He would then call Katherine Fairchild and tell her of his decision to participate in the bachelor auction. His mind wandered. It was funny—when he had told his mother about the auction and his initial reaction to it, she had said that he ought to do it and that he might find it fun. She was the third woman in one day to say the same thing.

Katherine's perfume, or rather his remembrance of the fragrance, still tickled his senses. It was a spicy, sexy scent without being overpowering. He still felt the warmth of her hand clasping his. All he had to do was close his eyes and a vividly real image of her face appeared before him—her exquisite turquoise eyes surrounded by those long dark lashes, her jet black hair framing the creamy smooth texture of her skin.

She had him confused. Aggressive feminists were not his type, and rich, pampered aggressive feminists were at the very bottom of his list. Yesterday, before he had met her, he had known everything about Katherine Fairchild he had needed or wanted to know. Today he found that he knew nothing about her and wanted to know everything.

As soon as he arrived at his office, Scott called Cheryl Johnston and set up an appointment for two that afternoon for his mother to meet with her. Cheryl seemed very pleased, especially when she heard Lynn's qualifications. Next, he placed a call to Katherine at the number she had left with him. The number belonged to the business office of the charity. He was disappointed that she had not been there, but he spoke to Liz Torrance and told her of his decision to participate in the bachelor auction.

He reached into his desk drawer and withdrew the sketch of Katherine that he had made. She represented everything he disliked in women; she was also constantly in his thoughts.

"Mrs. Blake, what a pleasure to see you again." Amelia's genuine affection for Lynn showed in her face.

"Hello, Amelia. It's nice to see you again, too. Is Scott in? I'm a little early for our meeting, but I thought we might be able to have lunch together."

"He's on the phone at the moment. He'll be right with you." Amelia always enjoyed Lynn's visits to the office.

The two women had become good friends over the years, each involved with a different facet of the same man's life. Now it was Scott who was their joint concern. They both agreed he should find the right woman and settle down, have a family. Lynn had, on more than one occasion, casually mentioned to him that she was the only one of her friends who did not have any grandchildren.

"Uh-oh, when the two of you get together, all of a sudden I'm twelve years old again." Scott's voice interrupted the casual conversation the two women were enjoying. The twinkle in his eyes said he was teasing.

"I know I'm a little early. I thought we might be able to have lunch together." Lynn nonchalantly brushed some stray blond locks from his forehead as she spoke. "If not, I have some shopping..." She turned her attention to Amelia, a thought suddenly occurring to her. "Why don't you and I have lunch together? We haven't done that in a long time. It'll be nice to have a chance for some uninterrupted conversation." She shot him a sly grin, then turned back to Amelia. "You can fill me in on what my son has been up to lately."

"Well," Scott chuckled as he spoke, "that was a quick about-face. You invite me to lunch and tell me I'm dismissed, all in one sentence."

"Would you like to go with us, dear?" Lynn gave him her very best look of innocence.

"Not a chance. One of you would tuck a napkin under my chin and the other would cut up my food—food you would order from the children's menu." Scott glanced at his watch. "Why don't you take two hours. I'll see you back here at one-thirty."

Lynn teased him as she patted him on the cheek. "You're a good boy. Your mother raised you right."

Scott rolled his eyes upward and slowly shook his head. In a pleading tone of voice he asked, "What did I do to deserve this?"

Amelia's face held a look of uncertainty. "Two hours for lunch, Mr. Blake? Are you sure that's okay?"

"Amelia, I'm the boss. At least, that's what it says on paper. I can make that decision. Now, the two of you, get out of here and enjoy yourselves." He escorted the two women out of Amelia's office and to the receptionist's desk. "I'll see you later."

As they waited for their food to be served, Lynn told Amelia about her appointment that afternoon at the Oakland center operated by the charity. Amelia was very pleased. "I knew that Ms. Fairchild would talk him into something. That's one very determined lady. A woman like that could easily fool a man, but another woman would see right through her. There's a lot more to her than he gives her credit for. In fact—" Amelia looked around the restaurant to make sure they could not be overheard, then lowered her voice to just above a whisper "—I think she'd be a good match for him—he just doesn't know it yet."

Scott opened the car door for Lynn while looking around the street, checking out the various boys "on duty." He did not see Billy anywhere, and immediately wondered if his car would be safe. He grabbed the paper bag from the back seat and tucked it under his arm before closing the car door.

"Cheryl, this is my mother, Lynn Blake. Mom, this is Cheryl Johnston. She's in charge of the Oakland operation and is in need of some first-class help in exchange for a third-class salary."

Cheryl shot him a quick look, then turned her attention to Lynn, extending her hand. "It's nice to meet you, Lynn. What Scott says is true, although I wouldn't have put it in quite those words."

Cheryl took Lynn on a tour of the facility, leaving Scott to fend for himself. His practiced eye quickly scanned the room, then came to rest on a mass of blond curls surrounding a tiny face with two big brown eyes peeking around the corner from the hallway.

He immediately sat down on the floor so he would not tower over the little girl. Then he reached into the paper bag and withdrew a teddy bear he had purchased while Lynn and Amelia were at lunch, and held it out toward the child. Using his most sincere smile and a soft voice, he called to her. "Hi, Jenny. Remember me? My name's Scott. I'm a friend of Kat's. I'd like to be your friend, too. I brought you a present. Would you please come over here and say hi to me? I'd like to see you smile. Kat says you have a pretty smile. Would you show me?"

He waited, remaining very still, as Jenny edged her way around the corner from the hallway into the main room. He continued to talk to her, his voice soft and soothing. He was very careful to make no sudden moves or gestures toward her. She slowly made her way across the room toward him, pausing to hide behind each piece of furniture she encountered before continuing.

Outside, Katherine Fairchild pulled up in front of the center, noting Scott's car parked at the curb. Cheryl had called her right after she had talked to him about his mother. Liz had called her right after she had talked to him about the auction. Katherine smiled to herself as she slid out from behind the wheel. There was no doubt in her mind that he would certainly get a big head if he had any idea how many people were standing by, awaiting any word from him. Everything was working out perfectly, even sooner than she had hoped.

Giggles and screams of delight greeted her as she opened the front door. Sitting cross-legged in the middle of the floor was Scott, with Jenny clutching the teddy bear and squirming in his arms as he tickled her. She felt the tears well in her eyes as she watched them laughing and playing together. If there had been any doubt in her mind about the type of person Scott Blake was, it was now banished forever.

"Kat...Kat." Jenny wiggled her way out of his grasp and ran to her.

"Hi, Jenny. Have you and Scott been having a good time together?" She wrapped the giggling little girl in her arms as she picked her up.

"Scott tickled me and made funny faces."

"What do you have here, Jenny?" Katherine indicated the teddy bear.

"Scott gave teddy to me."

"Oh, he did, did he?" She flashed him a grin as he quickly rose to his feet. He tried to hide his face from her, but not fast enough. There was no question in Katherine Fairchild's mind that he was embarrassed at being caught playing with Jenny.

"Well, uh, my mother and Cheryl are...uh—" he motioned in the direction they had gone "—touring." He was unable to make eye contact with her and desperately wanted to change the subject as quickly as possible. "I called the office this morning and talked to someone named Liz Torrance. I told her I had decided to participate in your auction."

As he talked he became aware of how she was dressed: designer jeans and sweater, Italian boots, very little makeup and her hair done in a French braid. The fashionably perfect socialite he had met yesterday seemed to have disappeared, somewhat. The clothes were still more fashionable than serviceable, but at least they were casual, rather than something out of this year's catalog of what the stylish pampered rich should be wearing. What surprised him most was her almost complete lack of makeup and the simple styling of her hair. For the first time he accepted the truth of how perfect, how flawless, her skin really was—what a truly beautiful woman stood before him.

He, too, had dressed in a manner more conducive to comfort. Yesterday he had had a business meeting with Brian Colgrave, which had called for a suit and tie. Today he was dressed in the manner more befitting his personality: what his mother called worn—he preferred to think of them as properly broken in—jeans and a brightly patterned sweater that set off his tanned face and blond hair.

"I'm pleased you decided to accept." She flashed him her most radiant smile. "Now I'm sure the event will be a rousing success. Have you given any thought to the type of date package you're going to put together?"

Scott walked over to where Katherine stood. When he reached her side Jenny stretched her arms out to him, wanting him to hold her. He took the giggling little girl from Katherine's arms.

"That was very interesting—" Lynn stopped in midsentence as she and Cheryl entered the main room and she spotted Scott holding Jenny and standing next to Katherine. A warm smile curled her lips. She immediately recognized Katherine Fairchild from the many news photos.

"Well, well, well—" Cheryl's amused voice broke the silence that had suddenly pervaded the room "—what do we have here? Jenny, who's your new friend?"

A small hand patted him on the nose, then on his cheek. "This is Scott. He tickled me and made funny faces." She held up the teddy bear. "He gave me teddy."

Cheryl directed her pleasure toward him. "I wouldn't have believed it if I hadn't seen it with my own eyes. You're some kind of a miracle worker, Scott."

Katherine reached over and tweaked Jenny's nose, causing the little girl to giggle again. "He's definitely the man of the hour." Her gaze settled on Scott's face as she placed her hand on his arm. "I wouldn't have believed it, either."

"Come on, Jenny—" Cheryl put her hands out to take the child from his arms "—it's time for your nap. Say goodbye to Scott."

Tears welled in her big brown eyes as she started to snif-fle. "I want Scott to tuck me in." She flung her arms around his neck and buried her head in his shoulder, re-fusing to let go.

Scott's gaze darted frantically from Cheryl to Kather-ine, then to his mother. He did not know anything about children and certainly nothing about little girls. He had not the vaguest idea of what to do or how to proceed. In a less-than-in-control voice he pleaded for help. "Will someone do something?"

Katherine seized the opportunity. "Of course Scott can tuck you in, Jenny." She grabbed his free hand and guided him toward the hallway.

The front door swung open with a loud crash as Billy burst into the room. "We got trouble!" His voice clearly conveyed the urgency of the situation. "Jenny's old lady and that bastard who beat her up are on their way here. You got a swift sixty seconds to hide the kid."

Katherine took immediate charge of the situation. She grabbed Jenny from a startled Scott and handed her to Cheryl. "Take her upstairs and keep quiet." Her gaze went to Billy, as if she knew what was about to happen. "Billy, put that knife away and get out of here."

Billy snapped the knife shut and jammed it back into his pocket. "I'm not leaving. I can take him out—" anger and hostility flashed in his eyes "—without the knife." Billy was not very big, only about five feet eight inches, but there was no room for doubt that he could handle himself in any kind of a fight.

"We've got a court order. Jenny's mother can't take her without going into court and proving she's fit to have cus-tody, and that will never happen. Now—"

The rest of Katherine's words were cut off by a surly male voice. "All right, give us back the kid so we can get out of here." The voice belonged to a man of about twenty, wearing dirty clothes and sporting green hair and one earring. He swaggered over to where Katherine stood. Following behind him was a small blond woman in her late teens, obviously Jenny's mother. She wore a too-short skirt with an incredibly low-cut blouse.

Katherine defiantly held her ground as she glared at the intruder. "I have a court order remanding Jenny to the custody of the center. You can't take her. Now get out or I'll call the police."

"Lady, I don't give a damn about your piece of paper. Wanda—" he jerked his thumb toward the blond woman "—wants her kid back."

Katherine's tone of voice clearly conveyed the disgust she felt. "Don't make me laugh. The only thing she wants back is the additional welfare money."

Scott quickly sized up Wanda's boyfriend. He was a little shorter than Billy and had a slight build. Any man who had to beat up little girls in order to make himself feel big was not going to take on a well-built man who stood six feet one inch and weighed 205 pounds. He saw Billy's hand slip back inside the pocket containing the switchblade. He quickly stepped between Billy and the intruder and casually put his arm around the man's shoulder. Offering his friendliest smile, Scott spoke to the intruder while steering him away from Katherine and toward the other side of the room. "There seems to be a little confusion here. Perhaps I can help straighten it out."

Those were the last words Katherine, Lynn and Wanda were able to make out. Scott's voice dropped so low they were unable to hear what he was saying. The smile remained in place and his hand stayed on the man's shoulder as he continued to talk. "We don't need to call the police. We can settle this very simply. I myself am a very easygoing type of guy. I'm not into violence. However, that intense young man leaning against the wall—" he indicated Billy, who was carefully following every word "—is ready to perform open-heart surgery on you."

Scott saw the quick look of uncertainty flash through the man's eyes as his gaze shot to Billy, then back to Scott, who was towering over him. "Now, we don't want to get involved in anything that messy, do we?"

As Scott continued to speak his fingers dug into the man's shoulder until he felt him flinch from the pain. "And then there're the ladies . . . we wouldn't want to upset them with a lot of unnecessary blood and violence. We won't even get into a discussion of who would be responsible for cleaning up what would be left of you. I can't speak for anyone else, but I don't care to dirty my hands."

Scott dropped his hand from the man's shoulder and stretched his height to the fullest as he looked down at him. "Now, why don't you and your girlfriend take a hike before this whole thing gets out of hand. There are things you can do to make up for the welfare money that's been cut off. You could try getting a job. . . ." Scott slowly scrutinized the man's appearance. "Of course, I can't imagine for the life of me who would want to hire you." The smile quickly disappeared from Scott's face and his voice became very menacing. "Do we understand each other?"

Scott watched as the man nodded. It was evident how uncomfortable the intruder was with the situation. He was alone, backed into a corner by one man who towered over him and another who was obviously street tough and had a knife. Scott flashed his smile again as he replaced his hand on the man's shoulder, giving him one last painful squeeze. He spoke at normal volume, loud enough for everyone to once again be able to hear him. "I'm sorry, pal, I didn't catch your name."

"Tom." The word was said without enthusiasm.

"Well, Tom. Too bad you and Wanda have to run along, but it was nice of you to stop by." Scott turned his head toward Billy as he continued to speak. "Aren't you going to say goodbye to our guests? We wouldn't want them to think we were rude."

"Naw, man. We wouldn't want them thinkin' that." Billy smiled as he sauntered over to where Tom and Scott stood. He clamped his hand on Tom's shoulder and gave it the same type of squeeze he had seen Scott administer. "Nice seein' ya, Tom."

Tom grabbed Wanda's arm and yanked her along behind him as he hurried out the door, turning to give one last furtive look in Scott's direction.

Scott turned a very serious expression toward Billy. "He's going to be back."

Billy returned his concern as he gave him a new look of respect and admiration. "Yeah, you're right."

Four

"**W**ould someone," Katherine intruded on Scott and Billy's conversation, "be good enough to tell me what just went on here? Why did they suddenly leave without another word about taking Jenny with them?"

"Oh, that." Scott tried to minimize the situation. "We—" he gave Billy a quick wink "—just explained the error of his ways. He saw the light and decided it was best for all concerned if they left."

Katherine leveled a cool look at Scott. "You're not going to tell me what you said to him?"

Scott feigned complete innocence. "Why, *Ms*. Fairchild—I just did. What more do you think there is?"

Her gaze shifted from Scott to Billy, who wore the very same look of innocence. "I see I'm not going to get anywhere with you two." She stepped to the hallway and called upstairs. "It's okay, Cheryl. You can come back down now. They've gone."

Cheryl quickly descended the stairs, carrying Jenny. She took a quick survey of the room, then turned to Lynn, who stood quietly taking in everything that had happened. "I hope this little incident doesn't discourage you. I think you'd be a real asset to our organization. I hope you decide to accept my offer."

Lynn looked around the room, her gaze resting momentarily on each person present. It seemed that everyone was waiting for her to say something. She glanced around the room one more time. "I taught high school English for twenty years. Over that period of time this type of incident, unfortunately, became an almost daily occurrence." She paused and noted the anxious looks being directed her way by everyone except Scott. His expression was one of knowing. "I could start tomorrow, if that's acceptable."

Cheryl let out a sigh of relief. "That would be perfect. Welcome aboard."

"Mom, let me introduce you to the rest of the people here. This is Katherine Fairchild."

The two women shook hands. "It's a pleasure to meet you, Lynn. This is quite a son you have here." Katherine shot him a quick grin. "Full of surprises."

Lynn beamed at him. "Yes, he is—simply full of surprises."

Scott could feel the flush rising on his cheeks. He stepped in to quickly change the subject. "Mom, this is Billy Sanchez. Billy, this is my mother, Lynn Blake. She's going to be working here, apparently starting tomorrow." He grinned at Billy, then turned back to Lynn. "You might want to give Billy a description of your car, including the license number. Unless, of course, you don't mind if it disappears off the face of the earth."

"So, you're Scott's ol' lady." Billy circled Lynn, carefully scrutinizing her. "You don't look old enough."

Lynn eyed Billy. Her voice did not hold any anger, but it did not hold any pleasure, either. "I'm his mother, not his 'ol' lady.' Other than that, thank you for the compliment."

Billy slowly nodded, then grinned at her. "You're okay."

What Scott had perceived as a tense moment had been satisfactorily resolved. With a sigh of relief, he addressed his comments to his mother. "I've got to get back to the office. Are you all set here?"

"Well..." Lynn hesitated.

Katherine quickly jumped into the conversation, directing her comments to Scott. "Why don't you go ahead and take care of your business? We've already taken too much of your time. I can give Lynn a lift to wherever she needs to go."

"Thank you, Katherine." Lynn was very pleased at the opportunity to spend some time alone with her, find out more about her.

A little voice broke into the conversation. "I want Scott to tuck me in." Jenny wiggled toward him, making it difficult for Cheryl to keep hold of her.

Scott looked at Cheryl with a "what do I do now?" expression. Cheryl held the child tighter and spoke softly to her. "Jenny, Scott has to leave right now. He can tuck you in some other time."

Jenny's big brown eyes brimmed with tears as her lower lip began to quiver. "I want Scott to tuck me in." A tear ran down her cheek as she held her arms out toward Scott.

Reluctantly, very unsure of what to do, Scott took Jenny into his arms and held her. He spoke softly to her. "I've never tucked in a little girl before. Can you tell me what to do?"

All eyes were on Scott as he carried Jenny upstairs. Katherine did not know what anyone else's thoughts were, but hers were definitely of a sensual nature. She allowed her gaze to wander over his handsome features, his broad shoulders and the way his jeans hugged his hips and long legs. *You may not have any experience tucking in little girls, but I bet you've had lots of experience with big ones.*

Scott may have been oblivious to the way Katherine's eyes followed his every move, but Lynn was not. Every nuance of Katherine's rapt interest was observed by her. Not only was she perfect for him, it appeared that she was also very interested in him.

Cheryl and Lynn went over Lynn's duties while Katherine busied herself with some paperwork. After ten minutes Scott came back down the stairs. He seemed slightly flustered, the expression on his face one of befuddlement and wonder. As he entered the front room he glanced back toward the stairs, then spoke. "She went right to sleep." He shot his mother a quick glance. "She wanted me to tell her a bedtime story—I don't remember any bedtime stories."

Katherine noted the flush of embarrassment rising on his cheeks. Her first impulse was to tease him about it, but she quelled the urge, saying instead, "I'm sorry to have imposed on you like that, but it was such a marvelous step forward for Jenny, I didn't want to stop the momentum." Her gaze stayed on his face, then captured his eyes. Her voice became softer. "Thank you for helping."

He was unable to pull his gaze away from her lovely turquoise eyes, which seemed to be looking right inside him, right through to his innermost thoughts. He found it unsettling; he found Katherine Fairchild unsettling. He finally stammered, "It was no trouble." He glanced around the room. "Now, if you'll excuse me, I need to get back to running a business."

After Scott left, Cheryl and Katherine continued Lynn's orientation on the inner workings of the charity, the other centers and functions, the educational program and the people involved. Katherine looked at her watch. "Oh, no, where has the time gone?" She glanced at Lynn. "I'm afraid we've kept you much too long."

"Not at all. It's been very enlightening."

"Well, I promised you a ride to wherever you needed to go. Are you ready?"

"Actually, Katherine, I live in Tiburon. I'm sure that's completely out of your way. I can take the BART, then the ferry to Sausalito, then the transit bus."

"I won't hear of it. Tiburon is certainly on my way. In fact—" Katherine thought quickly, trying to come up with a reason to spend more time with Lynn "—a friend of mine has been raving about a new restaurant in Sausalito, insisting that I give it a try. Tonight would be an ideal time. Could I persuade you to join me for dinner?"

Lynn was thrilled with this unexpected turn of events. "I'd be delighted."

The two women dined at an elegant little restaurant on the waterfront. The evening went by comfortably with both of them enjoying the beginnings of a genuine closeness. They chatted amiably about art, travel, music, current events—even sports and politics. The time passed much too quickly.

As Katherine pulled the car into the circular drive at Lynn's house, Lynn gathered her jacket and purse, then turned toward Katherine. "Won't you come in for a cup of coffee?"

Katherine immediately accepted the offer. "I'd love to."

"Make yourself comfortable—I'll be right back." Lynn went to the kitchen.

Katherine looked around the room, felt the love and closeness of the people who had lived there over the years. She picked up photographs and studied them. The only photographs in her house when she was a child were formal family portraits. These were snapshots taken of people having fun and enjoying their time together.

She could not remember their family ever taking a vacation together or doing family things just for fun. Her parents would go on trips, leaving the children with a governess and housekeeper. She was usually packed off for a month during the summer to someplace where the properly brought up little girls of the prominent families were sent, someplace they called "camp" but that bore very little resemblance to a place where kids played, got dirty and in general had fun. Only her grandfather had ever tried to give her any semblance of a normal childhood.

Tears sprang to her eyes as memories of her unhappy childhood flooded into her consciousness, memories that for many years she had kept locked away in the deepest, darkest recesses of her being, where she would not have to think about them, let alone deal with them; the loneliness, the humiliation...the beatings. She quickly recovered her composure when she heard Lynn returning from the kitchen.

Katherine pulled her car into her garage. Thoughts and feelings circulated through her being, thoughts and feelings of a warm happy home and a warm and caring mother. Scott was a very fortunate man. It had been a long time before she had overcome her own feelings of guilt, humiliation and anger. As a result she had always remained distant and reserved with all the members of her family—all except for her grandfather. Even now, time spent with her father or her brothers was stiff and awkward, very uncomfortable.

Her father had been too busy with his work to notice. Too busy to pay attention to his children and too busy to pick up on the desperate cries for help from a wife slowly sinking into an emotional abyss. It had been her grandfather who had first become suspicious about what was happening. It had been her grandfather who had saved her life—perhaps not literally but certainly figuratively.

When it had become known that her mother had been abusing her, that she was not just an accident-prone child who was constantly tripping over this or running into that, her mother had committed suicide rather than face the shame and retribution. That had only compounded the young Katherine's feelings of guilt.

Her mother had told her she loved her and the punishment was for her own good. Surely she must have deserved the beatings, or why else would her mother have administered them? Then, when her mother had taken her own life, she knew that had to be her fault. It was because she had finally allowed her grandfather to wheedle the truth out of her, when she had promised her mother she would never tell anyone what had happened. And then, for several years afterward, she had harbored the most sinful guilt of all; she had been relieved when she found out her mother was dead. It was a terrible load of guilt for one little girl to have to shoulder. Then there was her ill-fated marriage...

She had finally come to the realization that to dwell on bad experiences served no purpose. The only thing to do with bad experiences was to learn from them and move on so that the mistakes were not repeated and the same experiences did not happen again. The good that had come from her painful childhood was her dedication to the charity. If she could help even one child who had been subjected to similar abuses or, through the charity's educational program, prevent another child from ever having to know those abuses, then it had all been worthwhile.

She shook the memories from her mind. The bad times were all behind her; they were history. She returned her thoughts to the interesting evening she had spent with Lynn Blake. She hoped she had not been too obvious with her questions about Scott—what he liked to do in his leisure time, the type of books and movies he preferred. Her eyes misted as she recalled the sight of Jenny snuggled in Scott's arms.

Carruthers opened the door and admitted Bob Templeton to the foyer. "Mr. Fairchild will be with you shortly."

"Thanks, Carruthers. I'll just wait in the garden room." The attorney proceeded directly to the back of the house, having been there numerous times. He glanced at his watch and decided three o'clock was an acceptable hour to fix himself a drink from the bar cart.

"Let's have it, Bob. You've had long enough to work on this. Let's see what you've found out." R.J. Fairchild maneuvered his battery-powered wheelchair into the garden room. "And as long as you're taking liberties with my bar cart, fix me one of those, too."

"You know what your doctor said—"

"I also know I've outlived my doctor and am forty years older than his son, who is my current doctor, and I'll still be around long after he's gone. That ought to tell you which one of us knows the most about what's best for me." R.J. displayed his typical gruff exterior. "Now, get on with your report."

"The guy comes up squeaky clean. Three parking tickets and two years ago one speeding ticket. He's a graduate of U.C. Berkeley, took over as president of the company when his father died. All stock in the company is held by Scott and his mother. She holds fifty-five percent and he holds the remaining forty-five percent and carries the title of president, as well as chairman of the board. The old man built the company from scratch into a very successful enterprise and operated it in an ethical manner. The son is doing the same.

"The family background indicates a very close-knit relationship." He leveled a meaningful look at R.J. "You know, the stuff that happy endings are made of." He continued with his report. "He's never been married—several affairs, but they were always handled in a discreet manner and apparently weren't very serious. Except for one, that is. He did apply for a marriage license five years ago, about the time his father died. He never got married. I don't know if there's a connection between the broken engagement and his father's death or if it was only coincidental. He doesn't seem to be involved with anyone in particular at the moment. The mother is a retired high school teacher and, as of yesterday, is working at Katherine's charity center in Oakland. I don't find any cause for concern.''

The features on the old man's face began to relax a little and a slight smile played on his mouth. "Okay. We just can't be too careful after that situation with what's-his-name—you know, that fellow she married. We can't have that happening again."

"R.J.—" the attorney looked at him disapprovingly "—you know how angry Katherine would be if she knew you were having this man investigated. She's not nineteen years old anymore. She's a grown, mature woman. You can't continue to treat her like a little girl." He knew his words were falling on deaf ears. He also knew how much R.J. Fairchild adored his only granddaughter, and he was the only person outside the immediate family who knew why her grandfather still tried to protect her.

Katherine pulled her car up to the curb, noting the three police cars blocking the street. She had gotten the call from Cheryl at five o'clock in the morning, had immediately thrown on some clothes and had driven straight to the center. She was still hazy about exactly what had happened. Apparently Billy had gotten into a fight on the front porch of the center and someone had been hurt—she did not know who. She hurried up the walk to the front door.

As soon as she entered the room she saw Cheryl talking with two policemen and Billy sitting in a chair with another policeman watching him.

As soon as Billy saw her he jumped up and the words burst from his mouth. "Hey, Kat. It was Wanda and that bastard boyfriend of hers . . . they came here to—"

"Shut up, Billy. Don't say a word until I get my attorney here."

"But I didn't do anything—"

"Shut up!"

Billy reluctantly took the hint and plopped into the chair, his face registering his displeasure at being ordered around. He scowled as he watched Katherine hurry directly to the phone without bothering to pause and talk with the policemen.

She hung up the phone and turned to the officer who appeared to be in charge. "Now, what's going on here?"

"I'm Sergeant Caswell and you're . . . ?"

"I'm Katherine Fairchild."

"Are you in charge of this place?"

"For the purposes of whatever is going on here I'm in charge. This center is run by the Coalition for the Prevention of Child Abuse and I'm chairman of the board of directors. Now, I repeat my question—what happened?" Katherine fixed a very determined stare on the sergeant and waited for him to respond.

"Well, it appears that this young man, who refuses to give us his name, was involved in a knife fight with person or persons unknown. Judging from the blood on the porch and the lack of any wounds on him—" the officer cocked his head toward Billy "—I'd say somewhere out there is a person who's been pretty badly cut."

Katherine looked at Billy, who shot her back a look of defiance mixed with just a hint of uncertainty. She returned her attention to the officer. "And where is this other person?"

"We're searching the neighborhood now. The amount of blood would indicate that the person involved will need to seek medical attention."

"Are you arresting Billy?"

"We're holding him until we at least can identify him, and determine exactly what went on here. Any further action will be determined at that time. We'll be taking him into the station. You say his name is Billy?"

Katherine's stern look said volumes. "Be very careful how you treat him, Sergeant Caswell. He's only seventeen years old and that makes him a minor." She was pleased with the quick look of caution that crossed the officer's face.

Sergeant Caswell had finally realized exactly who Katherine Fairchild was and, as is often the case with the rich and famous, he backed off a little, especially since she had already called her attorney. Everyone knew who the Fairchild attorney was and everyone knew Bob Templeton was the best in the business.

Bob Templeton arrived at the center, unshaven and dressed in a pair of jeans and a sweatshirt. "Katherine, what's all this about?" He pulled her aside and they had a quick conversation.

Bob Templeton quickly converged on the officer in charge. "Sergeant Caswell, I'm Bob Templeton and I will be representing this young man. You are aware, I believe, that he is a minor and should be treated as such. Now, have you already questioned him?"

"I know who you are, Mr. Templeton. I've questioned him, but he hasn't answered me. He refuses to identify himself or give a statement about what happened here."

"If you will excuse me, I wish to confer with my client in private." Without waiting for a response from the officer, he quickly grabbed Billy and took him into the far corner, with Katherine joining them.

"Billy—" she spoke with a sense of urgency "—this is Bob Templeton and he's going to be your attorney. Now, tell us exactly what happened here and don't leave anything out."

Billy Sanchez looked at Katherine, glared at Bob Templeton, sat in silence for a long moment, then reluctantly started to talk. "It was Wanda and that Tom guy. I caught him trying to break in and we got into a minor scuffle." He saw the expression on Katherine's face, but before she could say anything he stopped her. "He ain't hurt that bad. I cut him a couple of times on the arm and he turned and ran like a scared rabbit." He sneered his contempt. "Anyone who'd beat up little girls doesn't have any stomach for a real fight."

Billy glanced quickly around the room, making sure no one could hear him. He lowered his voice to a mere whisper as he reached into his shirt pocket and pulled out a piece of paper. "He dropped this."

He handed the paper to Katherine, who scanned the words. Her anger set in as she clenched her jaw and handed the paper to Bob Templeton while filling him in on Jenny Hillerman and the incident that had happened just a few days ago.

"Who else was present during that confrontation?"

"Myself, Billy, Wanda and Tom, and Lynn Blake and Scott Blake. I sent Cheryl upstairs with Jenny before Wanda and Tom came in the door. Lynn is a new employee here at the center and—"

"Yes, I know who the Blakes are." Bob had spoken too quickly. As soon as the words were out of his mouth he knew he should not have said them. It was an inexcusable thing for an attorney to do—speak before thinking.

Katherine's eyes widened and her expression was a combination of surprise and anger. She said only one word, but that word said it all. "Grandpa!" She reserved her irritation long enough to fill Bob in on who Billy was and how he related to the center.

"Okay, Katherine. I'm sure I can get him released to the custody of the center with you as the responsible party. With all the reputable witnesses to the previous incident and the court evidence regarding Jenny, I'm sure there won't be any problems. However, I'm also pretty sure the judge is going to say that Billy either gets a job or gets back in school as a condition."

"Hey," Billy quickly interjected, "I didn't do nothin' wrong. Why am I being treated like someone convicted and being put out on parole? Why the conditions?"

"Because regardless of why this happened and who was the responsible party, that switchblade of yours is still a concealed weapon and illegal." He fixed Billy with a stern look. "You're not out of this yet."

Scott pulled up in front of the center. Lynn's car was in the shop and he had offered to take her to work. Both were immediately apprehensive at the sight of the police cars. Scott noted Katherine's car parked at the curb.

"Scott!" Katherine spotted him as soon as he walked in the door. She warmly acknowledged Lynn's presence but went immediately to Scott. She quickly filled both of them in on what had happened, then introduced them to Bob Templeton.

Bob terminated the conversation. "It looks like everyone is through here. They're taking Billy in. I should have him out in a couple of hours, then we'll come back here and discuss this job-or-school situation." Bob followed the officers out the door.

Even though the note had been given to the officers as evidence, Katherine vividly saw every word in her mind: *If you want to see the kid again get $5,000 and leave it in a paper bag on the front porch at midnight tomorrow night.*

Katherine told Scott exactly what the note said. "And only five thousand dollars...." Her voice became very soft, almost reflective. "I would have paid a hundred times that much."

"I'm sure they had no idea of the potential. Both are obviously uneducated—high school dropouts living on welfare. They weren't kidnapping a member of a prominent family—they were snatching her daughter from a charity center. I imagine that five thousand dollars seemed like a great deal of money to them."

"It was obvious that Billy caught them before they could grab Jenny." She turned an anguished face toward him. "I don't understand how someone could do this...."

He tried to make his voice teasing, tried to lighten the tension. "Well, *Ms.* Fairchild, I'm sure with your pampered, sheltered upbringing there are lots of things—"

Her anger flashed at him as she cut his words off cold. "How dare you presume anything about my upbringing! You don't know what you're talking about." She quickly turned her face away from him.

Scott was momentarily shocked by what had just happened. It was certainly not the reaction he had anticipated. He grabbed her arm to halt her as she turned away from him. "Kat?" He was not sure what to say. "I'm sorry if I've upset you. I didn't mean to presume..."

Her voice was filled with the agony that engulfed her. "Forget it." She tried to pull her arm away from his grasp.

He lightly brushed his fingertips across her cheek, then lifted her chin until he could look into her eyes. He saw it all—the anger, the pain, the fear, the vulnerability—as it crossed her face and was reflected in her eyes. His voice was soft and caring. "I don't think I can forget it." He wanted to reach out to her, take her in his arms and protect her from everything. This strong, assertive woman suddenly seemed so fragile to him, so in need of someone to take care of her. "Katherine?"

A silent moment of intense emotion passed between them as they stood together. His gaze never wavered as he tried to see inside her soul, tried to read her thoughts. He watched the embarrassment come into her eyes as she finally looked away. Then he gently lifted her chin again with his fingertips and turned her face back toward him. "What's wrong?"

"Nothing...it's nothing." She pulled away from his all-too-tempting touch. She wanted him to enfold her in his embrace and hold her. She wanted him to make the hurt and anger go away. "I guess I'm just a little tired."

He again turned her face toward him and studied her for a long moment. "You may be proficient at a great many things, Katherine Fairchild, but lying isn't one of them."

Her voice was soft, a mere whisper, as she pleaded with him to release her from his spell. "Please, I..."

"Why don't we go get some coffee—come to think of it, why don't we go and have some breakfast? Bob and Billy won't be back for a couple of hours and I think you could use a break." He smiled encouragingly. "Come on."

"Well, I guess so...." She glanced around and saw Cheryl, Lynn and two other employees involved with the day's scheduled business. Her expression brightened. "It looks like I'm not really needed here right now."

"Good. Give me a minute to call my office, then we'll go." Scott made a quick phone call to Amelia, then turned back to Katherine. "Are you ready?"

He placed his hand in the middle of her back as he gently guided her out the door and toward his car. Neither of them said anything as he drove to Jack London Square. Each was lost in his or her own thoughts. Curiously enough, each was thinking of the other person rather than of himself or herself.

Scott wondered what had been the hidden reason for her outburst when he thought it had been obvious that he was teasing her. The emotions that crossed her face and settled in her eyes tugged at his insides. He had not seen or talked to her since his mother had had her interview at the center, but Katherine was all he had thought about. Much to his dismay, she consumed his every waking minute.

Katherine knew she had overreacted to his simple teasing. She had become accustomed to his adding the extra emphasis to *Ms.* whenever he addressed her, but she had not been prepared for him to attack her background, to bring up her childhood. She immediately chastised herself for her thoughts. He had not attacked her background; he had merely tried to lighten the atmosphere. She really should apologize to him.

After they were seated at a table, had placed their order and been given coffee, Scott finally spoke. He decided to stay clear of the subject that had upset her so much. "What happens with Billy now? What was that business about a job or school?"

She began to relax as she filled Scott in on everything that had taken place and what Bob suspected would be the outcome for Billy. "I'm not sure how it can all be managed. I've tried several times to get Billy to go back to school, but he flatly refuses. He says he's not about to sit in some classroom with a bunch of kids five years younger than he is, and frankly, I don't know who would be willing to take a chance on giving him a job."

Katherine became momentarily lost in her own thoughts. The feel of Scott's warm touch as he placed his hand on top of hers brought her back to the reality of the moment. She slowly laced her fingers with his, the sensation sending tiny shivers of excitement through her body. A shy smile tugged at her lips as she looked into his eyes.

He saw her exposed vulnerability, felt the softness of her hand, experienced the warm sensation that melted inside him. Somewhere deep in his unconscious being he knew he had been caught—hook, line and sinker. His words were soft and sincere. "I think I might know someone who would be willing to take a chance on him."

Her eyes grew wide with anticipation. "Who?"

"Me." It was all that needed to be said. He saw her eyes glisten as they misted with happiness. He was definitely a goner—there remained only the formality of her reeling in her catch and his putting up a fight so that his capture would not appear to have been too easy, even though he instinctively knew that any struggle on his part would be to no avail.

Five

___

Scott and Katherine arrived at the center immediately after Bob Templeton returned with Billy. Bob addressed his comments to Katherine and Billy while Scott listened. "Billy has been released to the center with you as the responsible party. There is a court date for next week. I've already talked to the district attorney and, with the note and the witnesses to the previous incident, we'll be able to get him off with only a short probation—and it will definitely be school or a job." He directed his next comment to Billy. "Do you understand that? Katherine is responsible for everything you do, so you'd better behave yourself."

"Yeah, man, I heard." Billy was obviously not very happy about having to be answerable to someone.

Katherine beamed at Scott, then turned toward Bob. "We have a job for him." Billy immediately perked up his attention as she continued. "Scott—" her voice radiated her pleasure as she turned a shy but sincere smile in his direction "—has offered to put Billy to work."

Billy jumped up, his tone of voice indicating his disdain for the idea. "Doin' what? Diggin' ditches?"

Scott fixed him with a stern look. "Doing an honest day's work for fair wages. I'm starting a new construction project in San Rafael, a shopping center. I have a trainee program that I run and you would fit right into it."

Billy was smart enough to know when to shut up, and this was certainly one of those times.

"One more thing." Katherine aimed her question at Bob Templeton. "Jenny—am I within my legal rights to take her home with me? As long as Wanda and Tom are on the loose she's not safe here. The court order says custody of the center, but since I'm on the board, does that extend to my house?" The anxiety she felt clearly showed on her face.

Bob gave her shoulder a fatherly squeeze. "Sure, I don't think there will be any problem." He saw the relief spread across her face as she smiled at him.

Things seemed to be well under control. Scott called to his mother, who was across the room at her desk. "Mom, what time do you want me to pick you up?"

Katherine immediately jumped into the conversation. "If you'd like, you can leave your car with Lynn and I can drop you back in town...or wherever you're going."

Katherine took care of some business while Scott gave instructions to Billy to meet him at his office at seven the next morning, ready to work. Then Katherine and Scott left in her car and headed across the Oakland Bay Bridge toward San Francisco.

"Do you want me to drop you at your office?"

"I've got a better idea. It's a beautiful, sunny day. Why don't you drop me at the yacht club?" He paused long enough to allow his gaze to slowly move along the entire length of her body and back up to her face. "That is, after we stop at your place so you can change into something appropriate for sailing and then we go to my place so I can do the same."

"Sailing?" Her surprise was evident. She took her eyes off the road just long enough to glance at him, trying to determine if he was serious. "You want to take off in the middle of a workday and go sailing?"

"You're a quick study, *Ms*, Fairchild." The teasing tone of voice was unmistakable. "That's exactly what I want to do. Is that a problem for you?" His expression turned serious as he reached out and brushed his fingertips against her cheek. "I thought you could use a little diversion. It's been a pretty hectic morning for you."

She held his look for as long as she dared while driving, then flashed him a wide grin as she turned her attention back to the road. "No problem at all, Mr. Blake. None at all." She headed the car toward her house.

Katherine pulled into the garage and preceded Scott through the side door into the house. They entered a utility room, then the kitchen. He followed her on through the dining room, past the living room, up a flight of stairs and into the den on the second floor. "Make yourself at home—I'll be right back." He watched as she ascended the stairs to the third floor.

Scott slowly and thoroughly took in his surroundings. The den was large and comfortable. It was sectioned off into areas of interest. One section included all the latest toys and gadgets as far as audio and video equipment were concerned; another area contained a pool table. There was a wood-burning fireplace tucked away in a cozy corner with a love seat facing it and several large pillows on the floor. He wandered out into the hallway, peered through opened doors and found a bathroom and what appeared to be a tastefully decorated guest bedroom.

Katherine's voice, calling down from the third floor, interrupted his inspection tour. "Feel free to look around if you'd like."

"Thanks, that's what I'm already doing." He went downstairs and checked out the living room. It was much more formal than the den. It carried the feeling of proper dinner parties attended by the upper crust of society. The dining room was the same way; he saw it as only the best crystal, silver and china.

The kitchen seemed more comfortable and was enhanced by a sunny breakfast nook in the corner. Beyond the kitchen, behind the garage area, were what appeared to be servants' quarters—servants' quarters that were obviously unoccupied. He found it telling that Katherine Fairchild did not have a live-in housekeeper. He went back upstairs to the den to wait for her; another five minutes and she made her appearance.

She noted the quick darkening of his silver eyes to a charcoal color as he blatantly scrutinized her from head to toe, then back again. A slight shiver of anticipation darted through her body as she became aware of his intense gaze tracing her every curve. For a brief moment she felt naked and vulnerable, even though she was fully dressed.

He tried to bring his composure under control. She stood there looking more delicious than anyone had the right to look. She wore a simple light blue T-shirt and crisp white shorts. Her arms and long shapely legs were nicely tanned. There was no doubt about it: Katherine Fairchild had the best-looking legs he had ever seen. Her hair was pulled back at the nape of her neck, the top hanging in feathered fringes around her face. She wore just a touch of color on her soft lips. His gaze lingered on those lips.

Katherine broke the awkward silence. "Well, I'm ready to go." She offered him a shy smile.

He tried to keep the conversation light as they drove to his house. He asked if she had ever been sailing and did she know how to sail. His sailboat was fairly simple to handle and he was expert enough to be able to sail alone, but it was easier with two people doing the work. He was pleased to learn that she was a good swimmer and experienced in the basics of sailing.

They pulled into his driveway and quickly entered the house. He excused himself and left her in the living room as he went to his bedroom to change clothes. She wandered around the room. It had the same type of comfortable openness as his mother's house. The room reflected his strong personality without being overbearing in its masculinity. It also reflected his love of the outdoors and nature. Lynn had told her of his keen interest in ecology and environmental issues.

She opened the sliding glass door and stepped out onto the deck that overlooked the water. She smiled as the sun warmed her face. It was indeed a beautiful day, and perfect for sailing.

He watched her for several minutes as she stood at the deck railing. He was having difficulty categorizing the many thoughts and feelings that ran through him. He had known more than his share of women, but none like Katherine Fairchild.

In fact, he had almost married Carol. They had set a wedding date and applied for the license. Then his father had suffered a heart attack and died, and his life had been instantly thrown into turmoil. His primary concern had become making a smooth transition into running the company, so that none of their clients would be inconvenienced or the business disrupted, and also seeing that his mother was all right. Carol had been neither accepting nor understanding of the situation, and she had not liked having to share Scott's time.

In retrospect he knew the marriage would never have worked out. She had been obsessed with the status things of the socially prominent: the restaurant where the cream of society dined; tickets to only prestigious functions, whether or not they were something she enjoyed; dropping important names as if they were people she actually knew— in short, being a society snob, even though she did not have the background to account for it.

The final straw had come when she had wanted to attend a new gallery opening that had been touted in the papers as a glittering social event. It was on a night when he had promised to help his mother go through some of his father's personal belongings, selecting certain items to give to various family members. It was something very personal and private for both Scott and Lynn. Carol had made an unreasonable scene, insisting that he go with her or they were through. She had lost.

But still, he had been temporarily dazzled by her to the point of actually thinking he had been in love with her, so at the time he felt he had been dealt a double blow of heartache: the loss of his father and the breakup of his engagement. His experience with Carol had also left him with a bad taste where the social conventions of the rich and famous were concerned. A lesser man might have folded under the extreme emotional upheaval that had torn his life apart, but his inner strength had carried him through the ordeal.

He continued to study Katherine. She was unique; she was... He allowed his thoughts to fade—or perhaps he shoved them away—before they crystallized into some sort of reality. He finally spoke, before the thoughts could return. "I'm all set."

His words broke into her moment of contemplation. She whirled around, startled back into the here and now. A quick, but silent, intake of breath passed between her lips when she saw him. He wore a pair of shorts and a tank top. His broad shoulders, hard chest and long muscular legs were all very tanned. He apparently spent a great deal of time outdoors, probably on his sailboat. He looked absolutely gorgeous, a fact that did nothing to quell the tremors of excitement that were becoming increasingly prevalent.

Katherine stepped in from the deck and closed the sliding door. "This is a very nice room. It has the same feel as your mother's house—warm and comfortable." A sudden embarrassment surged through her and she quickly lowered her eyelids, her gaze coming to rest on the floor somewhere between them.

She sensed him standing in front of her, felt the overwhelming power of his closeness. He placed his fingertips under her chin and lifted her face until their eyes met. His sensuality engulfed her until she felt absolutely helpless. The sensation both frightened and excited her. Her breathing quickened ever so slightly.

"You seem to have difficulty with sincere personal moments—they seem to make you uncomfortable." His voice was soft and caring. He was neither teasing her, nor criticizing the embarrassment and shyness she tried to hide inside herself. He continued to hold her gaze as anxiety shivered through her. "Why is that?"

She did not know how to answer his question; she did not know if she even wanted to answer his question. He was trying to pry into feelings, fears and insecurities that had taken her many years to overcome. She used to keep them buried deep inside her but had finally learned to bring them out in the open and deal with them. She no longer found them frightening; she understood what they were about and where they came from. It was so seldom she was caught off guard or at a loss for words, but Scott Blake had a knack for crashing right through her exterior and getting to the heart of the matter. It was unsettling. Scott Blake was unsettling.

"I..." She pulled away from his tantalizing touch and regained her composure. "I really don't know what you're talking about." She flashed him a dazzling, although practiced, smile. "I thought we were going sailing?"

The day was unusually warm, and San Francisco Bay sparkled in the sunlight as the sleek sailboat moved gracefully through the water and passed under the Golden Gate

Bridge on its way out to the open sea. Katherine Fairchild
was still an enigma to him. It was more than her good looks
and sensual throaty voice that aroused his senses. She was
intelligent, poised, had a delicious sense of humor and an
independence that he found enticing—all in complete con-
trast to his preconceived notions. He found himself at-
tracted to her directness, her dedication to what she
believed in and her passion for what she felt was right. He
also noted she was hiding a shyness that was at odds with
the persona she projected.

She kicked off her deck shoes, stretched her legs out in
front of her and leaned back on her elbows. Her breasts
rose and fell with her breathing, the soft fabric of her shirt
clinging to the delightful fullness of her curves. His
thoughts were interrupted by the enthusiasm of her voice
and words.

"What a beautiful day, Scott! What a perfect day for
sailing!" The breeze ruffled through her hair, causing several strands to tickle her cheek. The sun warmed her face as
she leaned her head back and closed her eyes. The cries of
the gulls mingled with the sound of the wind in the sails.
She felt content . . . and at that moment very happy.

"Penny for your thoughts."

Scott's voice interrupted her moment of quiet reverie.
She opened her eyes and raised her hand to shade them
from the bright sun. "Oh, I was just thinking how perfect
everything is at this moment. I have to hand it to you. This
was a marvelous idea."

"I'm glad you're enjoying it."

It was almost five hours before they returned to the yacht
club to dock the boat. Both had wanted to stay out longer,
but she reminded him that she had to get back to the center to pick up Jenny. She did not want to leave the little girl
there overnight. They walked to her car in the parking lot.

"I can make it home from here. You'd better get going
or you'll wind up in the middle of the evening traffic snarl."

He reached his hand through the opened car window and ran his fingertips across her cheek. "Thanks for going sailing with me. I really enjoyed the day."

"Thanks for asking me. I really enjoyed it, too." Tremors of excitement shot through her being as he touched her cheek. Her breathing increased and her pulse quickened ever so slightly.

Their eyes locked in a moment of incendiary desire as he took her face in his hands and leaned toward her. Their lips brushed lightly, then he captured her mouth with his, the intensity of his passion consuming her.

Katherine Fairchild was totally lost. She had been anticipating this moment—if she could call a burning desire to feel his lips pressed against hers merely anticipating something. Perhaps feeling anxious about the inevitable moment was a better way of describing it, for she had known it would only be a matter of time. If he had not taken the initiative, she knew she would have thrown restraint and propriety to the wind.

His kiss was magic, his mouth sensual. She melted under the heat of his passion. Her hand, with a life of its own, reached out and caressed his cheek as she returned his intensity. Her heart pounded and the blood surged through her veins. She wanted Scott Blake. She wanted him body and soul.

Her lips were soft and she tasted so sweet. He had tried not to do this, but he had been unable to restrain himself. He had wanted to kiss her from the moment he had stepped into the elevator at the Hyatt and found her there. Every time he saw her only heightened the desire. This was not a good time or a good place, but he could not wait any longer to sample her delicious mouth.

He felt the heat of her passion as she returned his kiss. He wanted to wrap his arms around her, enfold her in his embrace. But with him standing in the parking lot leaning against her car and her sitting in the car, it was physically impossible. He slipped his tongue between her lips and twined it with hers as he explored the private recesses of her mouth. He did not want this to stop.

She welcomed the feel of his tongue touching hers. She did not want to leave, did not want this to stop. However, it had to stop, at least for now. She needed to be on her way back to Oakland to get Jenny. Slowly, reluctantly, she withdrew from the tantalizing web he was weaving around her. The words came out haltingly; her voice quavered. "I have to go... have to get Jenny... need to leave." She saw the smoky passion burning in the charcoal depths of his eyes.

"I know." His voice was soft and held just a hint of huskiness. He felt her tremble as his hand caressed her smooth cheek. He looked into her eyes and saw a startling sensuality tempered with just a touch of caution. "Have dinner with me tomorrow night."

They locked into each other's gaze, neither wavering. "I'd love to."

"Good. I'll call you tomorrow afternoon. Will you be at the center?"

"Yes."

Scott watched as her car moved down the street, around the corner and out of sight. He walked the few short blocks from the yacht club to his house, his thoughts filled with the soft sensuality of Katherine Fairchild.

Katherine's every thought and breath centered on Scott Blake. It had taken all her conscious effort to pull away from his kiss. He had caused tremors to shoot through her body, caused her breathing to quicken and her pulse to race. She had already made one big mistake where men were concerned. Did she dare to entertain thoughts of a serious relationship, to allow herself an emotional involvement rather than just a physical one? Could she trust her feelings and emotions? More important, could she overcome the bitter taste left over from her brief marriage? Would she be able to open her heart to love? She smiled inwardly as a feeling of calm pervaded her being. She was no longer that nineteen-year-old girl. She had learned, had grown and had overcome the major obstacles of her life. She knew the answer to all those questions was an emphatic *yes*.

Her thoughts snapped into the reality of the present. As soon as she picked up Jenny she would go see her grandfather. She had a few words to share with him about his having Scott investigated. She was torn between her anger that he would do such a thing to her and her knowledge of why he had done it. She knew that, in his own way, he was saying he loved her and wanted to protect her. She felt her anger subside—she just could not stay mad at him, no matter what he did. She was, however, going to let him know exactly how she felt about it.

"Kat!" Cheryl called to her as soon as she stepped through the front door of the center. "Sergeant Caswell is here to see you. I told him I didn't know where you were, but I was sure you'd be back here soon."

"Miss Fairchild—" Sergeant Caswell flipped through his small notebook "—we've gotten a line on Wanda and Tom. Someone answering his description went to an emergency medical-care center across town. The doctor fixed him up and told him to come back tomorrow so he could check on the stitches and change the dressing on the wound."

Her face lit up at the news, her enthusiasm evident in her voice. "That's great. Do you think you'll be able to arrest them?"

"When we catch up with them we will definitely be arresting them. Attempted kidnapping, and if the DA doesn't think he can make that stick, then there's extortion. One way or the other they'll be put away."

"Thank goodness. Then Jenny will be safe. I'm taking her home with me tonight."

"Now, Billy Sanchez—a court date has been set." He flipped the pages in his notebook, not noticing the questioning look Katherine shot at Cheryl and Cheryl's shrug in response.

Katherine quickly interjected, "He's doing some errands for me right now. He has a job and will be starting work at seven in the morning."

Sergeant Caswell looked up from his notebook, a momentary hint of surprise in his eyes. "Oh? Where will he be working?"

"He has a job with Blake Construction and will be working at the site of a new shopping center in San Rafael."

"And this can be verified with Blake Construction?"

"Absolutely. Scott Blake personally gave Billy the job. Billy is to report to Mr. Blake's office at seven."

After making the new entries, he closed the notebook. "That seems to take care of my business. Thank you for your time, Miss Fairchild. I'll keep you apprised of the status on Tom and Wanda." The officer then left the building.

Katherine rushed to Cheryl. "You don't know where Billy is?"

"I haven't a clue. Lynn might know. She was the last one talking to him before he took off." Cheryl glanced at the clock. "She said she had a personal errand to take care of— she should be back in a few minutes."

Katherine packed an overnight bag for Jenny and brought it downstairs. She immediately spotted Lynn coming up the front walk and rushed to talk to her. "Do you know where Billy is? Sergeant Caswell was here asking about him."

Lynn gave her a reassuring smile. "Yes, he's taking care of some personal business. He's just fine. He'll be spending the night here. In fact, he'll be staying at the center until all of this is finished."

"I've been trying to get him to stay here for a long time. How did you manage to talk him into it?"

"I didn't. It was his own idea." Lynn saw the relief on her face.

"As long as that's settled, I'd better get Jenny and go. It's almost her dinnertime." Katherine went into the next room and came back with Jenny, who held tightly to her hand while hugging her new teddy bear.

Katherine pulled her car up to the front door of R.J. Fairchild's house. Carruthers opened the door and she entered the house, Jenny clutching her hand.

"Grandpa, this is Jenny." The little girl hid behind Katherine's leg, peeking out to look at him. Katherine stooped and pulled Jenny into her arms. She spoke very softly to the child. "Can you say hello to Grandpa?" She watched as the child took a tentative step toward his wheelchair.

"Hello, Jenny. It's nice to meet you." The old man's voice took on a soft quality. In fact, his entire being took on a soft quality not normally part of his demeanor.

Jenny took a second step, then looked back at Katherine who gave the little girl an encouraging smile. She slowly made her way to the side of his wheelchair, then reached out her hand and patted his arm.

Katherine's eyes glistened with tears of pleasure as she watched R.J. Fairchild pick up the little girl and sit her on his lap. Jenny patted the side of his face and giggled.

The old man seemed genuinely enchanted with her. He pushed the control on the wheelchair and started toward the back of the house while talking to her. "Come on, Jenny. Let's take a ride to the garden room and see all the pretty flowers."

With a forthright honesty and openness that only children in the innocence of childhood possess, Jenny asked the powerful patriarch of the Fairchild empire, "Do you know how to make funny faces?"

He chuckled softly as they proceeded down the hallway. "I know how to make grumpy faces, but it's been a long time since I tried to make a funny face."

"Scott makes funny faces."

"Now, who is Scott?"

"He's my friend."

Katherine watched and listened to the exchange, the happiness welling inside her until she thought she would burst. *Who is Scott, indeed. The irascible old coot—he'll soon find out that he doesn't fool me for a second.* She would confront him about the investigation, but not now. She followed them down the hallway, the happiness she felt radiating from her face.

Jenny fell asleep on the couch in the den following dinner. Katherine took the opportunity to have the private conversation that had been the primary purpose of her visit. "Grandpa, I want to know why you had Scott Blake investigated." She could tell from the surprised expression that darted across his face before he could hide it that she had caught him completely off guard. It pleased her; it meant she had the upper hand for a change—at least, for the moment.

R.J. ignored her question, pointing to Jenny sleeping on the couch. "What an adorable child! I can see why you're so attached to her."

"No, you don't, you sly old fox. You're not going to wheedle your way out of this by changing the subject." She gave him a stern look that quickly changed to one of dismay. "How could you do this to me, Grandpa? How do you think Scott would feel if he knew about this?"

He saw the hurt in her eyes and realized he had gone too far this time. "Well, Katherine, perhaps I did overstep the boundaries just a bit—"

"Just a bit? How about clearly trespassing, meddling in something that's none of your business, treating me as if I were no older than Jenny? How could you do this to me?" She was almost in tears.

He knew he was undone. There was nothing that upset him more than seeing Katherine cry, knowing that she was unhappy—especially when he was the cause of it. He reached out and took her hand. "I'm sorry, Katherine. I guess I do tend to be a little overprotective. I just don't want to see you hurt again. Forgive me?"

She softened. He had done it again. She could not stay mad at him. "You know I do." She kissed his cheek.

"If it's any consolation, the report gives him a clean slate—first class all the way." He offered her a smile of confidence, hoping the information would please her.

"Speaking of the report, I want all the copies you have. I know it will be safer in my hands. Now—hand them over." She waited patiently while he reluctantly went to his desk and removed a file folder. She looked at it; printed on the tab in large block letters was Scott Blake.

She shoved the file folder into her large shoulder bag, said goodbye to her grandfather, picked up the sleeping child, carried her to the car and drove home.

She started to put Jenny into the guest room, then hesitated. What if she woke up during the night, was all alone and did not know where she was? She would probably be frightened. Katherine took her upstairs and tucked the little girl securely into her own bed. She reached into the shoulder bag and removed Jenny's teddy bear. She smiled warmly as she thought of Scott buying it, and she carefully placed it under Jenny's little arm.

Katherine bent and gave the sleeping child a loving kiss on the cheek, then smoothed her hair back from her face. "Good night, Jenny. May the rest of your life be filled only with pleasant dreams." She turned out the light and left the room.

She hesitated a moment after pulling the file folder out of her shoulder bag. She started to open it. Her grandfather had said Scott had a clean slate, first class all the way. Her curiosity overcame her reticence and she flipped open the report and started reading. Halfway through the first page she abruptly closed the folder and tossed it onto her desk.

No, she would not pry into his background. It had taken a lot of time, not to mention the thousands of dollars spent with the analyst, for her to retrieve her self-esteem from the place she had buried it, a place so deep inside her that it had been almost too painful for her to dig it out. But dig it out she had. She had learned to trust her emotions and instincts, to be strong. She would not allow the old feelings of insecurity and uncertainty to get a new foothold.

The night air was chilly, sending a shiver across her skin as she stepped out onto her deck. She was still dressed in her shorts and T-shirt, even though the sun had been down for several hours. She sipped her glass of wine as she reflected on the events of the day. What had started out as an absolute disaster before it was even daylight had turned into the most marvelous of afternoons. Scott was everything she had ever wanted, everything she needed. She closed her eyes and allowed images of Scott Blake to dance across the screen of her mind.

Six

Scott walked home and waited for his mother to return his car, then he took her to the garage to pick up her own. They discussed the events of the morning.

"Billy is really looking forward to working for you. He'll never say so, but I can see it in his eyes every time he mentions it. What are you going to have him do?"

"I thought I'd just turn him over to John Barclay. I called John while I was waiting for you and filled him in on the situation, and he's okay with it. He's the foreman on the project and in the best position to know where Billy would work out. Besides, he has a son about Billy's age, which might give him some insight into Billy. I've asked him to keep the circumstances of Billy's employment confidential. There's no reason for the entire crew to know."

"I'm real proud of you, dear. This is a very nice thing you're doing."

"Come on, Mom. It's no big deal. The kid's had a rough go of it and deserves a break. Besides, I'm not giving him anything—I expect him to work for his money just like any other member of the crew.''

She reached over and brushed an errant lock of hair from his forehead. ''It looks like you picked up some sun today. Did you go sailing?''

''Yeah, I went out for a few hours. It was too nice a day to pass up.''

Lynn smiled knowingly. ''I thought so. That would certainly explain the way Katherine was dressed when she picked up Jenny.''

He groaned and shot his mother a quick glance, then a wry grin. ''I can't have any privacy, can I?''

''I wasn't prying, dear—just observing.''

Scott settled into the corner of the living room couch with a book. After ten minutes he closed the book and set it aside. It was no use. He had read the same page several times and still did not have the vaguest idea what it said. He found it impossible to concentrate on the book when he kept seeing Katherine's face superimposed on the page— her sparkling turquoise eyes, finely sculpted features and absolutely delicious mouth. He could not speak for her, but that kiss had scorched him all the way down to his toes. He wondered how it was possible for that delightful package of brains, beauty and sensuality to still be single.

Scott was in his office very early the next morning to sort through the paperwork that had accumulated on his desk during his absence the day before. Amelia had rescheduled his only appointment. Other than that, it had been a light day. By the time he had finished organizing his desk he heard someone in the outer office.

''Billy, is that you?''

''Yeah.'' Billy sauntered in. ''So, this is where you work.'' He eyed the surroundings, taking in everything, then turned his attention to Scott. "You just sit up here and push paper around a desk?"

Scott suppressed a grin. He knew Billy was way out of his element and trying his best to be nonchalant, to not let anyone know he was impressed with what he was seeing. "Sometimes I'm in meetings or out at one of the construction sites. You're going to be working at a site in San Rafael where we're starting construction on a new shopping center."

A sudden thought struck him and he looked at Billy carefully. "How did you get here this morning?"

Anger flashed through Billy's eyes before he snapped, "What difference does it make? I'm here and I'm on time."

"You hitchhiked, didn't you?" Scott fixed him with a hard stare, refusing to break eye contact.

Finally Billy turned away, his voice much quieter. "Yeah, I hitchhiked. So what's the big deal?"

"I can't have you trying to bum a ride from Oakland to San Rafael every day. There's no way of guaranteeing that you'd be on time for work." Scott reached into his pocket and took out two twenty-dollar bills and one ten-dollar bill and handed them to Billy. "Here, take the BART from Oakland, then catch Golden Gate transit to San Rafael. Be glad you don't live in Los Angeles, where it would take you half a day to get that far on their bus system. Besides, you'll have to have lunch. You can't work all day on a construction project without lunch."

Billy glared at him defiantly. "I'm not takin' no charity. I told you I'd be to work on time and I will be."

"Charity? Not a chance. I expect you to pay back every penny of this fifty dollars out of your first paycheck." Scott shoved the money into Billy's shirt pocket. "Now, let's go, or you'll be late for your first day's work."

For a long moment Billy stood staring at the floor. He finally looked up at Scott, then turned and headed out the door, the money still in his pocket. Billy did not need to say a word; Scott saw it all in his eyes. No one had ever given him a break before and he did not know how to show his appreciation, how to respond to the situation.

On the way to the construction site Scott filled Billy in on how things would work. He would report directly to John Barclay and John was the only one who would know the circumstances of his employment. After getting Billy situated Scott went back to his office.

Katherine busied herself in the kitchen by fixing breakfast for Jenny. She was glad she had decided to move the little girl into her bedroom from the guest room. Twice during the night Jenny had awakened from a bad dream and Katherine had been right there to comfort her and see that she got back to sleep okay. Breakfast was almost ready, and Katherine went to check on Jenny in the bathtub.

The child giggled as she blew the bubbles off her hands. Katherine helped her out of the tub and dried her off. She started to help her dress, when Jenny informed her that she was a big girl and could dress herself. Katherine kissed Jenny on the cheek and waited as the child struggled with the clothes.

Everyone's day went along in an orderly manner. Billy was a little surly at first but finally settled into the work to be done. When the lunch break came he disappeared and no one knew where he went, but he was back on time to resume work. By the end of the day John was very pleased with Billy's efforts; he was working hard and making a genuine attempt to get along with the other crew members.

Katherine dropped Jenny back at the center, then hurried off to a luncheon meeting with a new potential corporate contributor. She planned to be back at the center no later than three o'clock, in time to get Scott's call about dinner. She paused and smiled softly as she thought about their dinner date that night.

Scott had a morning meeting, the one that had been rescheduled from the day before. Other than that, he found it difficult to keep his mind on the business at hand. Once projects were actually under construction, past the planning stages, his work load slowed down. Now was one of those times. He had two major projects in progress and several small jobs. Everything seemed to be going smoothly—it was, indeed, a marvelous world.

It was seven o'clock when Scott pulled up in front of Katherine's house. He had made reservations at Ernie's for dinner and was wearing a new suit. He felt excited at the prospect of spending the entire evening with her, and then afterward...well, perhaps nature would take its own course.

"Cheryl!" He was genuinely surprised to find her standing on the other side of Katherine's front door.

"I'm staying with Jenny while you and Kat have dinner." She greeted him warmly and stepped aside so he could enter the house. "Tom and Wanda are still on the loose and Kat doesn't want to leave Jenny at the center overnight until they're in custody."

"Scott?" Katherine's voice floated down from somewhere upstairs. "I'll be there in just a minute. I want to get Jenny settled in bed."

A little voice cried out, the excitement unmistakable. "Scott, Scott... I want Scott to tuck me in."

He glanced at Cheryl, who chuckled and shrugged. "I guess you've been summoned." She pointed up the stairway. "Third floor."

Jenny ran across the bedroom toward the door when she heard him coming up the stairs. "Scott...Scott."

He knelt as the giggling child ran to him and threw her arms around his neck. He picked her up and rose to his feet as he glanced casually around the room. This was Katherine's bedroom. It was tastefully decorated, a soft feminine quality without being frilly. It seemed to him that the entire third floor was a kind of separate area from the rest of the house. He noted the deck, a door that opened into a bathroom and another door that opened into what appeared to be an office.

Then his gaze fell on Katherine. She wore a turquoise silk dress that brought out the color of her eyes, the hem falling just above her knees. Her high heels were dyed to match. Her lustrous black hair was piled high on her head in the same manner as the first time he had met her. An elegant diamond necklace adorned her neck, and she had on matching earrings to complete the look. His breathing increased ever so slightly. He felt the excitement sizzle across the expanse of the room.

He carried Jenny across the room and gently deposited her on the large bed. "I want to go with you." Big brown eyes looked up at him, questioning eyes, wide with innocence.

He pulled the covers up around her. "You can't go tonight, Jenny. But—" he looked at Katherine "—tomorrow is Saturday. Maybe we can all go on a picnic. Would you like that?" He was not exactly sure to whom he was addressing his remarks, Katherine or Jenny.

"Doesn't that sound like fun?" Katherine sat on the edge of the bed next to Jenny. She casually brushed the little girl's blond curls away from her face. "Would you like to do that, Jenny?" Katherine allowed her gaze to travel to Scott's face, then her eyes locked with his. She saw the same smoldering charcoal intensity she had seen the day before. It sent shivers up her spine and caused butterflies to flit about her stomach in wild abandon.

"A picnic, a picnic!" Jenny's excitement sounded in her voice and showed on her face.

"Then that's what we'll do." Katherine bent over and kissed the giggling child on the cheek. "You be a good girl for Cheryl tonight."

"This is lovely, Scott." Katherine placed her fork on her plate after taking the last bite of her dinner.

He could not take his eyes off her. The flickering candlelight created soft dancing shadows that played over the silky texture of her skin. They held each other's gaze for a long moment, lost to the powerful depth of feeling that had been building between them all evening.

The spell was broken when the busboy cleared the dishes and the waiter inquired about dessert. Katherine and Scott both declined, claiming to be too full. Then Katherine glanced at her watch. "I really hate to put an end to this evening, but it's getting late and I need to let Cheryl get home. Her husband is probably fit to be tied by now."

They relinquished the table and left the restaurant. Scott pulled up in front of her house and turned off the engine, then reached his arm around her, pulling her to his side. "Thank you for having dinner with me." He ran his fingertips across her cheek and down the side of her neck. She tilted her face up toward his; her eyes sparkled and her lips were slightly parted. He lowered his head and captured her mouth, tasting the same sweetness as before.

Katherine's pulse raced as her breathing quickened. She was lost, totally under the spell of his magnetic sensuality. No one had ever made her feel the way he did, touched her very soul the way he was touching it at that moment. She reached her arms around him, running her fingers through his thick hair where it lay across the nape of his neck.

She returned all the passion of his kiss as her tongue twined with his. Wild surges of desire swept through her body; her heart pounded and her breathing became labored. His mouth was soft and sensual and at the same time insistent. She gladly gave everything it demanded.

It was Scott who finally broke off the kiss. His voice was thick, his breathing ragged. He cupped her face in his hands and looked intently into her eyes. "I feel like a teenager making out in the car. Any minute now your father is going to flip the porch light on and off as a signal for you to get inside the house." He touched his slightly trembling fingertips to her kiss-swollen lips, let out a soft groan, then released her from his embrace.

He opened the car door for her and held out his hand to assist her. He continued to hold her hand as they walked to the front door of her house. After unlocking the door, she turned to him. "Would you like to come in for an after-dinner drink?"

"I'd like that very much."

Katherine called out as they entered the house, "Cheryl, we're back." They went upstairs to the den.

Cheryl came down from the third floor. "I was just checking on Jenny. She woke up earlier, another bad dream."

A slight frown wrinkled Katherine's brow and a look of sorrow clouded her face as she slowly shook her head. "I was hoping they would have stopped by now. The poor little thing, she still doesn't feel safe and loved." A faraway look came into her eyes as she said in a whisper, more to herself than to anyone else, "I wonder if she ever will." She knew how long it had been when she was a little girl before she had been able to sleep the night through without the nightmares returning, how much time had passed before she had completely buried the pain, only to have to resurrect it again with the analyst. A resurrection, however, that had been worth every minute of having to relive every painful memory.

Scott heard the anguish in her whispered words and remembered the anger, the pain, the fear and the vulnerability that had crossed her face and been reflected in her eyes when he had tried to tease her about her pampered background. He slipped his arm around her shoulders and gave her a comforting squeeze. He did not know what she was hiding, but whatever it was, it had hurt her deeply.

"Well, I'd better get home before Dan locks me out." Cheryl grabbed her jacket and purse from the table.

Scott immediately started for the stairs. "Let me walk you to your car. It's late and it's dark out."

Cheryl smiled graciously. "That's most gallant, sir, but it won't be necessary. Good night." She headed down the stairs and out the front door.

Scott took off his suit jacket, draped it across the back of the love seat and loosened his tie before sitting down.

Katherine's eyes sparkled as she watched him; her tone of voice teased him. "Feel free to make yourself comfortable."

He patted the seat cushion next to him as his look captured hers. "Why don't you come and sit down?"

Shivers shook her as she moved toward the love seat. Her words were playful, but her heart pounded and her breathing had quickened. "Oh? Are you getting ideas?"

"No, I'm not getting them—I've already got them."

There was nothing subtle about the sexual tension that permeated the room. Both of them felt it. Both of them were drawn into it. It was like a whirling vortex that trapped anything and everything in its path. She felt light-headed as he reached out and grasped her hand, drawing her down next to him.

Neither of them spoke; words seemed so unnecessary, seemed almost an intrusion into the sensual veil that enveloped them. His mouth seized, nibbled, devoured—he could not get enough of her sweet taste. He wanted her, all of her. Nothing else mattered at that moment.

"Mommy...Mommy..." Jenny's screams ripped through the house, instantly dowsing the heated passion that had been rapidly building between them.

Katherine jerked to attention. "Jenny!" She pushed away from Scott and ran from the room. Her heart pounded, but not from her inflamed desires. Jenny was having another nightmare. She knew very well what the nightmares were. They were the same type that used to make her wake up screaming in the middle of the night. She knew how frightening they were for the little girl.

Katherine sat on the edge of the bed, wrapped her arms around Jenny and gently rocked her. "It's okay, Jenny. I'm here with you—you're not alone." She continued to hold the sobbing child.

It had all happened so fast. One moment he had had a soft, sensual and very desirable woman in his embrace who was driving him into a frenzy, and the next moment he was alone. Scott stood at the bedroom door, watching Katherine rock Jenny in her arms. She continued to talk to the child in whispers. She was oblivious to his presence.

"It's okay, Jenny. No one is going to hurt you. You're safe." A look of pain and anguish crossed her face, then changed into a hardened determination. "I know what's happening inside you, what you're going through. I know about the nightmares. I promise you no one will ever hurt you again. I won't let them."

Her words jolted him. He did not know what to make of them, how to interpret their meaning. There were too many loose pieces surrounding Katherine's life and he was unable to put them together. He watched as she continued to hold Jenny in her arms and rock her, even though the little girl had stopped crying and appeared to be sleeping again.

"Is she okay?"

Scott's voice startled Katherine. She had not been aware that he was in the room, did not know how much he had heard. "Yes, she's sleeping." She tucked the covers around Jenny. The little girl looked so peaceful and angelic—no one would ever suspect that she had just been through a nightmare.

He took Katherine's hand and led her from the room. "Are you okay?"

"Me? Why, of course!" His question unnerved her. She did not know what had made him ask it. She felt his fingertips under her chin as he lifted her face. And now he was staring into her inner being, looking into her soul. Then his lips were on hers—not the demanding passion of earlier, but instead a soft, gentle caring.

"You're a very special lady, Katherine Fairchild." He looked into the depths of her eyes for a long moment, searching for some sort of answer to his unasked question. Finally he spoke again. "Why don't you and Jenny meet me at my house about ten-thirty tomorrow morning? We'll take the ferry to Angel Island and have our picnic."

"We'll be there."

Scott retrieved his coat. The mood and the sensual spell had been broken. He reluctantly left her house.

Billy slammed the book closed. "Jeez, I can't do this. It's no use."

Lynn Blake gave him a stern look. "Yes, you can. All you have to do is apply yourself. You're obviously smart—you'd have to be to have survived on the streets since you were thirteen without getting into drugs or ending up in reform school. Now, young man—" she tapped the cover of the book "—get to it."

"Mom?" Scott called from the front room as he walked through the house toward the kitchen.

Billy quickly shoved the books and papers across the kitchen table and jumped to his feet. "Jeez, what next?"

"In the kitchen, dear," Lynn answered.

"I need to borrow..." Scott's voice trailed off as he saw Billy.

"Borrow what, dear?"

A frown tugged at Scott's forehead. "I'm not interrupting anything, am I?"

"Not at all. Billy volunteered to help me with a few things. We were just discussing what needed to be done."

Scott noted the quick look of relief that crossed Billy's face. Lynn offered no further explanation and Billy said nothing, so Scott decided to let the matter drop. "I want to borrow the picnic basket—" he glanced down at the floor "—and a picnic lunch to go with the basket."

Lynn's eyes sparkled with unconcealed amusement as she looked at her son. "A picnic lunch? For how many people?"

"Two...no, three...actually, two adults and one child." Not only was his mother amused with the situation, but Billy was clearly enjoying Scott's embarrassment.

Scott carried the picnic basket and Katherine held Jenny's hand as they boarded the ferry that would take them to Angel Island, a state park located in San Francisco Bay. He had been surprised at the way she was dressed—a pair of old, faded jeans, a T-shirt and sneakers. Her hair was fixed in a French braid and again she wore only a hint of makeup.

She seemed very far removed from the proper socialite who had confronted him in his office that first morning. He marveled at how she had touched his life, how their lives had become so interconnected, how she caused things to happen. She had actually persuaded him to participate in the bachelor auction.

He had been trying for a long time to get his mother out of the house and involved in something, and now she was working at the center—a job she had told him she found very fulfilling. Billy was working for him at one of his construction sites and was apparently helping his mother with something. Life was, indeed, strange.

When they got to the picnic site, Scott spread the blanket out on the ground under the tree. They had decided against the picnic table, preferring what Katherine had called "an old-fashioned picnic." After lunch they took a walk along one of the wooded trails. The sun filtered down through the trees, creating mottled patterns of light and shadow on the ground. The gentle breeze rustled the leaves.

He held Katherine's hand as they strolled along the path. Jenny would run ahead of them, hide behind a tree, jump out and say, "Boo!" then giggle and run ahead again.

"Oh, Scott, for the first time in her life she can run, play and laugh—the way all children should." A look of sadness covered her face. "I wonder what's going to happen to her, if she'll ever have a permanent home and a family to love and care for her."

It was the same look he had seen on her face before. He squeezed her hand, then brought it to his lips, kissing the back of it. "I'm sure she'll be fine. She has you, doesn't she?"

Katherine gave him a shy smile, then leaned her head against his shoulder as they continued to walk.

Twenty minutes later Jenny snuggled in the picnic blanket as Katherine handed her the teddy bear. Not only was it past time for her nap, she was completely worn out from the romp in the woods. Scott had carried the little girl back to their picnic site. In a matter of moments she was sound asleep.

After Jenny was settled, Scott sat down with his back against a tree and his long legs stretched out in front of him. Katherine sat between his legs, her back against his chest, his arms around her waist and his cheek against her head. She rested her hands along the outer edges of his thighs. Neither spoke for a long time as they enjoyed their closeness.

She felt so comfortable with him, being in his arms felt so right. She allowed her mind to wander back to the previous night—to where things might have gone if Jenny had not had the nightmare that had put an end to their heated moment of passion. She had engaged in a few, discreet, physical relationships since her divorce, but none in which she had made much of an emotional investment. But this was different, very different. She knew being with Scott would be something very special. She also knew that being with him forever was what she wanted most.

Katherine was not the only one thinking about the previous night. Scott had hardly thought of anything else. Her passionate response to him was beyond his expectations, was more than he had hoped for. She filled his every waking moment. It shocked him to realize how quickly everything had happened. It had been only a week, but he felt as though he had known her a lifetime. What shocked him even more was the realization that he wanted it to be a lifetime.

A little more than two hours passed before Jenny woke up from her nap. The moment went unnoticed by Katherine and Scott, who were both involved in the delicious sensations of a romantic kiss—as romantic as possible in a public place in the middle of the day. Their idyll was broken by the sound of a tiny voice saying, "You guys are kissing," followed by a series of giggles.

Katherine turned out the lamp, then sat on the edge of the bed, pulling the blanket up around Jenny's shoulders. It had been a long day for the little girl, one filled with exciting new things. After they rode the Angel Island ferry back to Tiburon, Scott had taken them for pizza. Then they returned to his house, where Katherine had left her car. Jenny yawned, trying desperately to stay awake so she would not miss anything.

The afternoon had solidified Katherine's feelings about Scott. He was her one burning desire in life. She found herself suddenly surrounded by all the things she had never had, all the things she had thought she would never be able to have, the things that money cannot buy—an intelligent, warm man whose mere presence filled her with excitement; his caring mother, to replace the mother she had never had; a child, a darling little girl, who really needed her.

In Katherine's entire life no one had ever really needed her before. No one, except her grandfather, had ever really even cared about her. She sat quietly on the edge of the bed and watched the little girl sleep. She hoped the bad dreams would not return that night. Then she kissed Jenny tenderly on the cheek and left the room.

The phone woke Katherine. She squinted at the clock— it was only five-thirty. She glanced over at Jenny—the little girl was still sleeping. She tried to clear the grogginess from her head. She had been having a highly erotic dream about Scott. With a voice still thick with sleep she got up and answered the phone. "Hello."

"Miss Fairchild?"

She did not recognize the man's voice. Her senses became immediately alert. "Who's calling?"

"This is Sergeant Caswell, Miss Fairchild."

A tremor of anxiety rocked her. "Yes, Sergeant Caswell, what can I do for you?"

"We need someone to make a positive identification—"

"Identification?" Her voice quavered and her body trembled.

"It's Tom and Wanda. They went back to the emergency-care center to have the dressing on his wound changed. One of our patrol cars spotted them. They were on a motorcycle and tried to get away. There was an accident...."

Her stomach churned and tied in knots as she listened to the rest of what the police officer was saying. "Certainly, Sergeant Caswell. I'll be there as soon as I can." She replaced the receiver in its cradle. For a moment she stood motionless, not quite sure what to do. She could not leave

Jenny alone and she certainly could not take the little girl with her.

She picked up the phone and dialed Scott.

Katherine dressed, being very quiet so she would not wake Jenny. She nervously paced up and down the kitchen, drinking coffee and waiting for Scott. He had agreed to come right over and watch Jenny for her. After what seemed an eternity she heard a car pull into her driveway. She rushed to the door.

"Lynn!" She stepped aside to let Scott and his mother come in.

"I brought Mom along. She's going to take Jenny back to her house and keep her there through tonight."

Scott had taken immediate control of the situation.

"Don't worry about anything. I'll bring her to the center in the morning when I go to work." Lynn gave Katherine a comforting smile and a little hug. "Now, show me where her things are."

Katherine looked perplexed. "Well..."

"I'm going with you. I don't want you doing this alone." It was not a question; Scott was telling her the way things were going to happen. "Show Mom where Jenny's things are."

Scott pulled the car up to Katherine's house. She had not uttered a word the entire ride back from the morgue. They entered the house and went upstairs to the den, where she collapsed onto the love seat and just sat there, as if in a daze. He sat next to her—putting his arms around her, pulling her next to him, giving her his strength and comfort.

She finally spoke, as much to herself as to him. "The entire time she's been at the center she's never once asked where her mother was or when she would be back. Only in her nightmares does she ever call out to her." She turned anguish-filled eyes toward Scott. "How can I tell her? How can I tell her that she will never see her mother again, that her mother is never coming back?"

Seven

Katherine's unanswered question hung heavily in the air. Scott felt her body tremble from the emotional turmoil as he held her close. "I don't know. Even if you found the words, would she understand? Perhaps it would be best if you waited. Give it a little time, for both of you."

She reached up and grasped the hand he had rested on her shoulder. She tried to bring back the words used to tell her that her mother was never coming back. Of course, she had been ten years old, much older than Jenny. To a three-year-old, death was an abstract concept, the understanding of which was not easily grasped. Perhaps Scott was right; maybe it would be better to wait for a while. She gave his hand a squeeze as she looked into his face, offering him a shy smile. "I'm sorry to have called you at such an awful hour, but I really appreciate your having insisted on going with me. I don't know if I would have been able to do that by myself."

"I'm glad you did call me." He kissed her on the cheek and held her in his embrace for a moment longer. "It's almost lunchtime, and I don't know about you, but I haven't had any breakfast. I didn't even get any coffee. How about we go out and get something to eat?"

"Why don't I fix us something to eat right here?" She slipped out of his arms and got to her feet.

"Brains, beauty and can cook, too? Why, *Ms.* Fairchild, how is it that some lucky man hasn't snapped you up before now?" His teasing grin spread across his face until he caught the look in her eyes. He held her look of uncertainty for a long moment. "Katherine? What's wrong?"

She reached her hand out toward him. Someone had "snapped her up"—someone who had turned out to be a cold, unfeeling gigolo who had used her, who had not really cared about her at all. She hastily withdrew her hand, dismissing the memory and regaining her composure. Her practiced smile quickly covered her face. "Nothing's wrong. I just think you should reserve your opinion about my cooking until after you've tasted it." She laughed. "You could be in for a rude awakening." With that, she turned and went downstairs to the kitchen.

Scott followed her. It had happened again—she was definitely hiding something.

After eating, they had taken their coffee up to the den. Katherine put some music on the stereo while Scott headed for the fireplace. The beautiful weather of just a few days ago had given way to a storm front. "It feels like it's going to rain. There's nothing like a cozy fire on a dreary day." In a matter of minutes he had the flames dancing over the logs in the fireplace.

Katherine seductively slipped her arms around his neck, stood on her toes and brushed her lips against his. "You're a very nice man."

His eyes widened in mock surprise. "Why, *Ms.* Fairchild, if I didn't know better, I'd swear you were trying to seduce me." His breathing quickened ever so slightly as she ran her hand across the nape of his neck and tickled her fingers through his thick hair.

She brushed her lips against his again, then softly teased, "Why, Mr. Blake, whatever would make you say a thing like that?"

Their gazes locked for an instant, then she removed her arms from around his neck and took a step back. He grabbed her arm and pulled her against him, holding her tightly. His voice was husky, thick with the passion that surged through him. "Don't start something that you're not prepared to finish."

She trembled in his arms as she rested her head against his chest. She heard his heart beating and felt his ragged breathing. Her voice was a whisper. "I was prepared to finish it Friday night. I'm still prepared." She felt his arms grow tighter still around her.

He closed his eyes and rested his cheek against the top of her head. "Oh, Katherine...I want to make love to you so very much." He held her closely for a moment longer, then brought his mouth against hers, filling her with his passion.

More than anything she wanted Scott Blake to make love to her. She melted in his embrace, savored the texture of his tongue against hers, trembled as his hands caressed her back and shoulders. Elation soared within her as she returned all the heat of his fervor.

In one smooth motion he scooped her up in his arms and carried her across the room toward the stairs. Her fingers went to the buttons of his shirt and unfastened them. By the time they had reached the top of the stairs she had his shirt completely undone. He released her from his arms, placed her on the floor next to the bed, then gently cupped her face in his hands.

Katherine saw the smoldering intensity of his ardor in his eyes. Did she dare to hope that those eyes also contained love? His mouth captured hers again, his kiss hot and exciting.

Like some sort of dream sequence in a movie, they slowly and sensuously undressed each other, pieces of clothing dropping to the carpeting one at a time. He laid her back into the softness of the large bed, then stretched out next to her, his hand caressing the length of her body before finally coming to rest over the fullness of her breast. His words were magic. "You are so beautiful, so exquisite. I want to please you so much."

She felt the heat of his inflamed desire every place he touched her bare skin, whether with his lips or his fingers. He trailed sensual kisses across her cheek and down the side of her neck. She arched her back to more fully press her body against his. Her arms encircled him, her hands caressing his broad shoulders and strong back. His tongue tasted the tempting skin between her breasts, then he kissed the underside of each one. He gently manipulated her nipples, teasing them to taut peaks.

Shivers of delight darted through her body and a soft moan escaped her lips as he drew her nipple into his sensuous mouth. As he gently suckled she ran her foot along his bare calf. Her breathing became labored as his mouth became more demanding. He was such a skillful lover. He instinctively knew each and every place to touch her, how to excite her senses to new heights of pleasure.

Katherine felt herself sinking into a mindless abyss. Nothing mattered except Scott and the wonderful things he was doing to her, the incredible sensations he was creating within her. There was no doubt in her mind as she gave herself totally and completely—she loved him; she loved him so very much. She wanted to be with him always.

Scott caressed the gentle curve of her hip, teased the dark downy softness at the apex of her thighs. He felt her entire body quiver as he slipped his hand along her smooth inner thigh. Her soft moans and whimpers of delight only added to the incendiary atmosphere that sizzled around them like a hot desert day.

He rolled her over on top of him. Her body was soft and supple, her skin silky. His fingers tickled down her back, then he caressed the roundness of her bottom. The swell of her firm breasts pressed against his hard chest as it heaved with his ragged breathing. She was the embodiment of everything he had ever wanted, everything he had been searching for all these years. He wanted to consume her, to possess her, to be possessed by her, to be part of her for all time.

"I should have asked earlier..." His voice was thick, the words difficult for him to formulate. "Is it okay? Are you protected?"

"Yes—" she felt his hardened arousal pressing against her stomach as she lay on top of him "—it's safe." Her voice was low. She was almost beyond the ability to think straight. He rolled her over onto her back again, his body covering hers. She trembled as he brushed his fingers through her downy triangle, then slipped a finger between the warm moist folds of her femininity.

"Oh, Scott—" His mouth came down hard on hers, cutting off her words. He gave to her as much unbridled frenzied passion as he demanded from her.

He inserted his knee between her thighs, gently parting them. Then, his body poised above hers, he slowly penetrated the heat of her passion with his burning desire. He heard her quick gasp as he entered her, felt her arms draw him nearer. A delicious thrill surged between them as he thrust deep inside her.

They immediately fell into a slow, smooth rhythm, her hips rising to meet his every stroke. They were so in sync, so attuned to each other. They achieved a rhythmic unison, a harmony of oneness. Each savored the sensual feelings, the growing tremors of excitement.

He captured her mouth, his tongue thrusting in coordination with the cadence of his hips. Her taste was as sweet as the first time he had kissed her, her lips as soft. His movements became more intense. He felt the rapture building deep inside him.

Katherine held him tightly. The convulsions started deep within her, causing her to cry out in ecstasy. Her being soared, her spirit sailed through the gossamer veils of rhapsody that enveloped her body and soul. Never in her life had she felt the way she did at that very moment. He was the center of her universe. She teetered on the brink of a huge chasm before plunging over the edge into a cloud of euphoria.

Scott could hold back no longer. With one final urgent thrust, his body stiffened, then he shuddered as the spasms overtook him. He buried his face in her neck, holding her tightly in his embrace. His breath came in hard puffs.

Their bodies glistened with a thin sheen of perspiration as they lay together in bed. He placed a soft kiss on her cheek. Neither was able to speak. They continued to hold each other in silence, their breathing slowly returning to normal. He stroked her hair, brushing back the loose tendrils that clung to the dampness of her face. He brushed his lips softly against hers.

The pounding of her heart finally slowed to normal. Her entire being rejoiced at his nearness, his touch. She had never felt so content, so at peace. She truly loved him very much.

He continued to hold her in his arms, reveling at her softness, cherishing her closeness. He had never before felt so at one with any woman. He wanted to stay in her bed, stay with her.

They basked in the golden afterglow of their intense lovemaking. They exchanged the murmurings of lovers, sensually and playfully touched each other, laughed together and tenderly held each other. It was a time of warmth and closeness combined with quiet reflection.

"Come away with me for the weekend—we'll find a romantic hideaway somewhere up the coast." Scott's words tickled her ear, causing shivers of excitement to race up her spine.

"You're forgetting the auction. The closer we get to it the more work there is to do."

He frowned. "It's not this coming weekend, is it?"

"No, it's three weeks from yesterday, but things are becoming hectic. This coming Friday night is the press conference and after that I'll be totally buried in the preparations for the event."

He kissed her on the cheek and allowed a teasing grin to cover his face. "Then you'll need a break—need to go away for the weekend and replenish your energy, relax before you wear yourself out."

She studied the honesty and openness of his face, which belied the smoldering intensity in his eyes. "This coming weekend is out of the question." Her manner became shy, hesitant—as if she was unsure whether her question was appropriate. "Do I have another choice?"

He nibbled at her earlobe and teased the corners of her mouth. "How about the weekend after that, the weekend between the press conference and the auction?"

Her answer was barely above a whisper as she traced the outline of his lips with her index finger. She knew she should not be doing it, that it was not the "responsible" thing to be doing at this time. She also knew it was what she wanted the most. "I'd like that—I'd like that very much."

Scott was in his office early the next morning, eager to face whatever the day had to offer. He had stayed at Katherine's house until almost five o'clock in the morning, leaving only to go home to get ready for work. He paused as the memory of their lovemaking flooded his mind. It had been very special. She was a warm, responsive, caring woman with a passionate sensuality that could melt anything.

His reflections were interrupted by the buzzing of the intercom. "Yes, Amelia."

"Liz Torrance is on the phone. She wants to talk to you about the auction."

Liz and Scott talked for almost half an hour. He provided her with the information on the date package he had put together. They talked about convenient times for publicity pictures and interviews and set up a schedule agreeable to both of them. Since the auction was so near at hand, everyone at the charity who was involved with its preparations would be very busy.

As soon as he finished his conversation with Liz, he turned his attention to a new project that had just come in. He needed to study the architect's plans, then spec out the materials required and do a bid on a twenty-story building. The request had come from George Weddington, an architect who had worked closely with Scott's father over the years and continued to work with Scott. He was the architect who designed all the shopping centers for the Colgrave Corporation, not just the one in San Rafael. As with Brian Colgrave, Scott had a very close working relationship with George Weddington, based on mutual respect and the desire to produce a quality product. He cleared his mind of all intruding thoughts and concentrated on the project at hand.

Katherine, too, had a busy day planned: a fund-raising meeting in the morning and an auction-planning meeting in the afternoon. She paused in her thoughts long enough to allow a warm glow to envelop her. She had never felt so alive. Just the memory of her lovemaking with Scott made her body tingle. For the first time she truly looked forward to the future and the excitement it held. She grabbed three file folders off the top of her desk and shoved them into her attaché case. She turned to leave her office, then halted long enough to brush all the other files cluttering her desk top into a desk drawer.

As soon as Katherine arrived at the Hyatt, Liz showed her the list of all fifteen participating bachelors and their date packages. It was the first hint she had of what Scott had planned. He had refused to tell her. She read his date-package report with keen interest. He proposed a weekend in Yosemite National Park, about a four-hour drive from San Francisco. He had reserved two rooms at the luxurious Ahwahnee Hotel in Yosemite Valley for the weekend following the auction, the first weekend in November. He stressed the nature and environmental aspects of the weekend, the assumption being that whoever bid on it would be someone who enjoyed the outdoors, walking the trails, communing with nature.

As Katherine floated through the finance meeting, Jim Dalton made particular mention of how radiant she looked. They discussed budgets for the various projects and allocated funds for specific items. Following the finance-committee meeting they broke for lunch before the auction meeting that afternoon. Liz excused herself from lunch so that she could take care of some personal errands.

"Lynn, over here." Katherine waved as soon as she saw Lynn step out of the elevator. She had asked Lynn to help with arrangements for the auction and the fund-raising party at her grandfather's house following the auction.

Lynn quickly crossed the lobby to where Katherine and Jim waited. "I hope I'm not late."

"Not at all." Katherine turned toward Jim. "Jim Dalton, I'd like to introduce Lynn Blake. Lynn is a former schoolteacher who was good enough to come out of retirement and accept our offer to work at the Oakland center with Cheryl. She also happens to be the mother of one of our bachelors." She turned toward Lynn. "Jim is a member of the finance committee and also on the board of directors. He's worked with us from the very beginning and we couldn't get along without him."

Jim's outgoing laugh cut into Katherine's words as he turned toward Lynn. "Yes, and next month I'm applying for sainthood." He extended his hand. "It's a pleasure to meet you, Lynn. Katherine has said many good things about you."

"The pleasure is all mine." Lynn returned his smile as they shook hands.

"Well, ladies, shall we grab some lunch?"

Katherine was very pleased with herself. She did not believe in matchmaking—she had suffered the efforts of her friends and business associates for years—but she really felt that Jim Dalton and Lynn Blake would have so much in common. When it was suggested that the committee could use another person to help with auction planning, she immediately offered Lynn's name. She had been very pleased when Lynn had agreed to take on the extra work.

Lunch turned out to be more fun than Katherine had anticipated. Lynn and Jim hit it off immediately. He regaled them with stories and anecdotes from the days of what he called his "reckless youth." Yes, indeed, Katherine was very pleased with herself.

The afternoon auction meeting was all business. Lynn contributed several good suggestions and the committee accomplished quite a bit. Following the auction meeting, Katherine drove directly to the Oakland center. As soon as she stepped through the door Jenny ran to her. She picked up the little girl, who seemed to be looking around for something—or someone.

"What's the matter, Jenny?" She gave the child a kiss on the cheek and smoothed back her bouncing curls.

"Where's Scott?"

"He's not here. He has work to do." The child squirmed so much that Katherine finally had to put her down.

Cheryl watched them with a teasing twinkle in her eyes. "Jenny was telling us about your picnic."

The little girl giggled. "They were kissing."

Katherine turned every shade of red known to man and nature plus some more, a situation not helped by the amused smiles of everyone at the center.

Katherine watched as Jenny left the room, then, in an attempt to change the subject as quickly as possible, she turned to Cheryl and spoke in a low, serious voice. "You are aware of what happened yesterday?"

Cheryl's manner became very professional. "Yes, I knew as soon as I saw Lynn arrive with Jenny that something was wrong. Sergeant Caswell called later this morning with the same information that Lynn gave me." She paused for a moment. "What happens now?"

"I guess..." Katherine's voice quavered. "I guess we need to find her a good home, a family who will want to adopt her." Her face took on a look of determination. "I don't want her in and out of foster homes. I want her to have a real home and a real family."

Cheryl leveled a cool, appraising look at her. "How about your home?"

Katherine held her look for a long moment but turned away without responding to Cheryl's comment. Jenny needed more than just a place to live. She needed a home and a family—both a mother and father who would be there for her, a house with a yard where she could play on a swing, a bouncing little puppy, a...

Scott left his office following a busy day. He had stayed late working on the bid for the office building. As he headed north across the Golden Gate Bridge his mind turned to Katherine Fairchild. She occupied more and more of his thoughts; if he was not concentrating on a specific thing, she was automatically there. On this particular occasion his thoughts turned to their weekend out of town together. He wanted it to be something very special.

He pulled his car into the driveway and was shocked to see Billy sitting on his front porch. Billy jumped up and started for the car.

"Billy! What are you doing here?" Scott opened the car door and quickly got out.

"Uh...look, there's..." Billy was obviously uncomfortable. All of Scott's senses were on immediate alert. Something was definitely wrong.

"Let's go inside." Scott unlocked the front door and entered the house.

Billy followed him and immediately slumped into a chair. Scott stared at him. "Okay. What's on your mind?"

"Well...you got some trouble at the construction site." Billy shifted uncomfortably in his chair, his gaze darting nervously around the room.

"What kind of trouble? You've only worked there two days, Friday and today. What do you know that I don't?"

Billy took immediate offense at Scott's words. "Hey, man. I know what I saw!" He glared at Scott but saw that the look directed his way was not one of reproach or criticism. He calmed down.

"All right, tell me what you saw."

Billy rose and paced around the room, finally coming to rest on the deck overlooking the bay. "You got a nice view here. Kind of like your ol' la—I mean your mom's."

"Thank you. Now, why don't you get to the point."

"Yeah. Well, uh, you got a couple of guys doin' drugs on the job."

Scott jerked to attention. He had always been very emphatic that anyone caught drinking on the job or doing drugs would be fired immediately, no exceptions. Everyone who worked on his crews had been apprised of that long-standing rule. "Are you sure about this?"

Billy's anger flared. "Yeah, I'm sure. They're also stealing stuff. Nothin' big—yet."

"Who else knows about this?"

"I ain't told no one, just you."

"Why didn't you tell John Barclay? He's in charge of the project and he's on-site all the time."

"Hey, I don't know him from nobody. He could be involved, for all I know." Billy paused momentarily to collect his thoughts. This conversation was very difficult for him, not part of the way he was accustomed to doing things. He glared at Scott for a long minute, then spoke in a calmer, more controlled manner. "I ain't no squealer. They don't bother me and I don't mess in their business, but they're stealin' from you and could be hurting the job. You've been straight with me—I just wanted to return the favor." He headed for the door. "I gotta go."

"Wait a minute. Who is it? What are their names?"

"I said all I'm gonna say. If you trust this John guy, then let him figure it out. It shouldn't be too tough if he just keeps his eyes open." With that, Billy slammed out the front door and hurried down the street.

Scott sat in stunned silence for several minutes, then moved to the phone and called John Barclay. "And, John, when we bust these guys, let's make sure we do it so that Billy has no involvement. Just tell them you've been on to them for a while and have been watching them. I know it's difficult to keep track of everything on a job that big, but first thing in the morning start a thorough inventory to determine exactly what's missing."

He listened to John's response, then replied, "You're right. That would be better. I'll have the inventory done by someone not connected with that project and claim it's part of an annual audit."

Having completed his business with John, Scott fixed himself some dinner. As he ate, his thoughts turned again to Katherine Fairchild and their upcoming weekend. He dialed her phone number but got only the answering machine.

Katherine poured herself a glass of wine and one for her grandfather. "My heart just goes out to her, Grandpa. She's only three and she's already been through more than some people go through in an entire lifetime. She needs a home and a family." She tried to suppress the sob that forced its way out of her and the tears that threatened to overflow her eyes. "Sometimes I just feel so helpless. I want so much for everything to be okay for her."

R.J. Fairchild studied his granddaughter. "You identify very closely with her, don't you?"

"Yes, I do. I don't want her to make the same mistakes I did. I don't want her to spend half her life wondering what she did to cause her mother not to love her. I don't want her to blame herself for her mother's death. I don't want her to have to wait until she's an adult before she understands and learns to deal with the reality of causes rather than just being controlled by the symptoms."

A quick look of anguish crossed her face. "I don't want her to be so desperate to have someone love her that she'll run off and marry the first person who pays even the slightest attention to her." *And then find out that all he ever wanted was a piece of the family fortune; that he was sleeping with anything in a skirt, including the person she thought was her best friend; that he was flaunting his infidelities in public and would only agree to a quiet divorce without a scandal and the harsh glare of publicity if he was paid a huge cash settlement.*

A cold shiver ran up her spine as a single tear trickled down her cheek. She would do everything she could to make sure that Jenny was protected from all the emotional upheaval she had been subjected to as a child. She would make sure that the little girl knew that someone loved her and cared about her.

It was late when Katherine arrived home. She checked her answering machine and there was only one call. She immediately recognized Scott's voice and his teasing tone.

"This is an obscene phone call. Since you're not there to receive this call in person, I'll have to be content with some heavy breathing." She laughed out loud as she heard his exaggerated panting. "If you find any of this even mildly stimulating, call me at my office in the morning and we'll see if we can't do something obscene together tomorrow night—I'd even be willing to buy you dinner first." There was a brief pause, then she heard his words, soft and caring. "Good night, Katherine. I..." He never finished his sentence.

She turned off the machine. Her eyes glistened with happiness. "Good night, Scott. I love you."

Katherine and Scott left the little Italian restaurant tucked away in a corner of the North Beach area. He slipped his arm around her shoulders as they walked toward the car. They enjoyed the comfort of their closeness; neither felt pressured to talk, nor awkward with the silence.

She turned to him as he pulled his car up to her house. "Would you like to come in for coffee?"

He ran his fingers across her cheek as his breathing quickened. "Did you really think you needed to ask?" He brushed his lips lightly against hers, then opened the car door. They walked hand in hand into the house.

As soon as they reached the kitchen he pulled her into his embrace. His voice was thick with emotion. "I don't really want any coffee."

Her words were a whisper. "Neither do I."

He took her hand and led her up the stairs to the third floor. They paused next to her bed. He cupped her face in his hands and studied her for a long moment. "I've never met anyone like you. I didn't think anyone like you even existed." He lowered his mouth to hers, infusing her with his deep feelings and emotions.

Katherine lay cradled in his arms as they luxuriated in the glow of contentment that enveloped them. Once again their lovemaking had been very intense, filled with the heated passions that flowed between them. She had never before known the depth of feeling or the height of rhapsody that he gave to her.

He kissed each delicately puckered nipple, then brushed his lips against hers. "I have to go to Los Angeles in the morning." His voice was soft as his fingers drew lazy circles across her stomach and abdomen. "I'll be gone tomorrow and Thursday. I'll get home late Thursday night. Have dinner with me on Friday." His fingers tickled along her inner thigh as his mouth captured hers. He felt her hand caress his reawakened arousal, her foot rub against his leg.

Katherine spent Wednesday and Thursday working on the publicity campaign for the bachelor auction. The publicity releases were out; a press conference had been set up for Friday afternoon.

On Thursday morning Katherine was in court with Billy and Bob Templeton. As Bob had predicted, with the circumstances surrounding the incident and a deposition from John Barclay about Billy's good work record, Billy was given three months' probation and the entire situation was kept as part of his juvenile record. Everything seemed to be progressing in a smooth manner. She was very pleased.

Friday morning found Scott at the construction site in San Rafael. He spent half an hour with John Barclay in the construction office trailer. After their conversation Monday night John had kept a watchful eye on all the crew members, especially those working in areas in proximity to where Billy worked. By early Tuesday afternoon he had spotted the two culprits working in an area fairly isolated from the rest of the construction. He kept a log of their activities. They appeared to be doing cocaine two or three times a day. On Wednesday morning a team of "auditors" showed up and began a thorough inventory.

Scott and John left the office trailer and walked briskly across the construction site. With few amenities and no pleasantries, Scott immediately dismissed the two workers. In accordance with company policy, he presented them with a written notice of termination stating specifically why they were being fired. Their final checks had already been drawn. Before the checks were handed over, the two men were required to countersign the personnel form stating that they had been presented with full documentation as to why they had been dismissed.

"Our attorneys will contact the police and provide them full details, with the possibility of criminal charges being made pending the outcome of the inventory." With those final words, Scott had security escort the two men from the site. He could tell from the looks on the men's faces that they were shaken to their boots and would not be back making any trouble.

John walked Scott to his car, giving Scott an opportunity to ask him how Billy was working out. John was thoughtful for a moment, then answered, "He works hard, keeps to himself, doesn't give anyone any problems. There's just one thing...every day at lunchtime he disappears. He's always back on time, but I have no idea where he goes or why. Another thing, on his first day here he asked around for anyone who could give him a lift as far as Tiburon each night after work."

Eight

Scott stopped by his house on the way from the construction site to his office. He needed to change into a suit for the auction press conference and knew he would not have time to return home that afternoon. His mind turned to Katherine. After the press conference they would go out to dinner. He had not seen her since he had left her house about midnight Tuesday. He missed her. It bothered him how much he missed her, considering he had only been out of town for two days. A frown tugged at his forehead as he drove south across the Golden Gate Bridge.

The press conference took place at the Hyatt Regency. Katherine stayed in the background while Liz presided over the activities—as would be the case with the auction, too. Scott was surprised at the number of reporters and photographers that were present. He had no idea that something like this would attract so much publicity. He felt uncomfortable, ill at ease with the cameras and questions. He disliked being on display.

He was particularly irritated with the reporter who asked him about his personal relationship with Katherine Fairchild, noting that they had been seen dining together in an atmosphere that was anything but businesslike. Scott was as tactful as possible while giving one of those "nonanswer" types of answers.

Scott loosened his tie as he and Katherine walked out of the hotel. "I'm sure glad that's over. I don't know how you deal with that constant glare of publicity, having your life continually held up to public scrutiny."

A sigh escaped her lips. "You get used to it after a while. You just have to learn not to let it control you, that's all." Her mind flashed back to the press conference. She could tell from watching Scott how uncomfortable he was, particularly when the questions had centered on their relationship. She wondered for a moment if the public spotlight would eventually cause problems between them, and shivered at the idea.

They claimed their own cars from valet parking. Scott followed Katherine home so that she could leave her car, then they went to dinner. He had picked out a charming French restaurant off the beaten path, where, he hoped, they would not be noticed.

They spent an enchanting two hours at the restaurant, mesmerized by the warm glow of the unspoken love that surrounded them. Katherine had never been so happy, truly happy, in her entire life as she was whenever they were together.

"Do you have any plans for tomorrow?" Scott clasped her hand as they walked to the car.

"I promised Jenny I'd take her to the zoo. Would you like to go with us?"

The weather was cool in spite of the sunshine. Katherine helped Jenny with her jacket as Scott pulled into the parking lot. The little girl was so excited she had hardly been able to sit still. She had kept up a constant line of chatter from the moment they picked her up at the center.

Jenny's eyes widened with wonder and awe as she craned her neck to look up at the giraffes. She giggled and clapped her hands at the antics of the monkeys. She kept repeating "big kitty, big kitty" when she saw the lions. Everything was fresh and new to her.

Katherine seemed to be as excited as Jenny, Scott thought as he watched them carefully. A warm feeling of contentment settled deep inside him. With Katherine at his side and the darling little girl discovering wondrous new things, he felt the missing pieces of his life had been found.

It had been a very busy day. Katherine tucked Jenny into bed in the guest room, then joined Scott in the den. "She went right to sleep—she was exhausted."

He flashed her a decidedly lascivious grin, his silver eyes shimmering with desire. "How would you like to tuck me into bed? Of course, I feel I must warn you—I don't think I'll be going right to sleep. I'm *not* exhausted . . . yet."

She tried to suppress the grin that threatened as she snuggled next to him on the couch. A warm glow radiated throughout her body when he slipped his arm around her shoulders and drew her closer to him. She covered his hand with hers and leaned her head against his shoulder.

They stayed together on the couch, enjoying the quiet moments. Neither spoke; just being together was enough. Occasionally Scott would lean over and place a soft kiss on her cheek or forehead.

"Mommy . . . Mommy . . ."

Jenny's screams pierced the quiet of the house. Katherine jumped to her feet and raced to the guest room. The little girl was having another of her nightmares.

"Jenny, precious, it's okay. I'm here with you." She wrapped the sobbing child in her arms and rocked her gently, assuming she would go right back to sleep.

Between sobs, Jenny asked the question for the first time—the question Katherine knew she would eventually have to deal with. "Where's my mommy?"

A hard lump formed in Katherine's throat and her mouth went dry. She had been dreading this moment, dreading the time when she would have to tell Jenny what had happened. Cheryl had volunteered to be the one to do so, and perhaps she would have been better qualified to handle the situation, but Katherine felt it was her responsibility. She wiped the tears from Jenny's cheeks and smoothed back her blond curls. Big, brown innocent eyes—innocent and frightened eyes—looked up at her.

"Jenny, honey...your mommy..." She desperately tried to remember exactly how her grandfather had told her about her own mother. She had asked her father, but he had not known what to say, so it was her grandfather who had taken the responsibility. It was her grandfather who had, once again, been her strength and lifeline. She had been ten when her grandfather had told her; Jenny was only three. She did not know how much the little girl would understand, but she had to try.

She hugged the child tightly against her body. "Your mommy has gone away and won't be coming back." She measured her words. "It's not because she doesn't want to come back—it's because she can't come back. Your mommy...your mommy was in an accident. She was hurt real bad...then she...she..." The words caught in her throat and she had to force them out. "She died."

She continued to hug the child closely to her. "Your mommy wanted to come back—she wanted to be with you again. Your mommy loved you. Always remember that— your mommy loved you and she couldn't help that she had to go away." She continued to rock the little girl gently in her arms. "I know what you're going through, Jenny. I know exactly. I know about the bad dreams. I know how frightening they are for you. They're just like the dreams I used to have." She paused as she took a steadying breath, then continued, talking as much to herself as to the child.

"It's not your fault, Jenny. It's not your fault that your mommy went away and it's not your fault that she won't be able to come back. You didn't do anything wrong." She looked into the innocent little face. "Do you understand that, my precious? You did not do anything wrong. It is not your fault. I love you, Jenny, and I won't let anything or anyone ever hurt you again. I'll always be here whenever you need me. Please believe me, I know exactly what you're feeling and what's happening to you. I know you don't really understand now because you're too young, but someday you will and then everything will be okay." Katherine hugged Jenny securely against her body as tears trickled down her cheeks, tears shed not for her own memories but for the uncertainty of Jenny's future.

Scott stood back from the bedroom door. He had listened to Katherine's words and had felt the emotion behind them. It was another piece of the puzzle that seemed to surround her life. He had been left with the distinct impression that she had been talking about herself as much as she had been talking to Jenny. He also felt that it was an important moment for Katherine and Jenny to be sharing, and as much as he wanted to provide comfort to Katherine and Jenny, he should not interfere. He quietly slipped away and returned to the den to wait.

Katherine continued to rock Jenny in her arms until the child was sound asleep. Then she lovingly tucked her into bed, kissed her forehead and left the room.

The weekend had gone by very quickly, too quickly for Scott. Time was moving too fast. There used to be time for everything, but not anymore. He leafed through his schedule book; the coming weekend he and Katherine were going away to a romantic hideaway, the following weekend was the bachelor auction and the week after that was the weekend of his reservations at Yosemite for the date package. And interspersed with those personal activities were numerous business meetings and an increasingly heavy work load.

Scott settled in at his desk. Amelia brought him a cup of coffee and the morning mail. The first order of business that Monday morning was a revision of the bid on George Weddington's latest project. He unrolled the new drawings and began studying them, comparing them with the old ones. It was going to be a long day.

It was late when he finally arrived home. As soon as he entered the house he noticed the envelope on the floor, obviously shoved under the door. It was the envelope that had contained Billy's paycheck. Inside it was a crisp new fifty-dollar bill, nothing else. Scott smiled to himself as he pocketed the money. The crew had been paid that morning; Billy must have gone to the bank immediately.

Even though it was late he placed a call to Katherine. He wanted to hear her voice before going to bed. They talked about the preparations for the auction, then about their upcoming weekend out of town. He refused to tell her where they were going.

The balance of the week was very hectic for both of them. They could not get their schedules to mesh. She had two dinner meetings on nights when he was clear; he had a meeting on the only night she had a clear schedule. They managed a quick lunch together, but that was the only time they saw each other. They talked on the phone each night— if only for a few minutes.

Friday finally arrived. Scott picked Katherine up that afternoon. As soon as he stepped into her house he pulled her into his arms. "It seems like forever since I've seen you. Last weekend went too fast and this week has gone too slow." Without giving her a chance to say anything, he captured her mouth with his, filling her with his longing and desire.

She trembled in his embrace as she willingly returned every emotion, every heated promise of what their weekend would hold. She had told her grandfather she was not looking for a husband, but more and more her thoughts were turning toward marriage and a family.

Katherine knew Cheryl had been right: her home was where Jenny belonged. But not just the two of them. Scott was the missing ingredient, the person who would allow them to be a real family. She wished she knew for sure how he felt. He said all the right things, but he had never told her he loved her. She more than wanted him; she needed him—very much. She and Jenny both needed him.

Scott headed the car north, then cut across to the coast. He had picked a charming inn at the Russian River as their final destination. Their room was spacious, contained a wood-burning fireplace and had a large deck with a breathtaking view of the spectacular coastline. An ice bucket and bottle of champagne had been placed in their room, per his instructions.

They stood on the deck overlooking the ocean. He held her hand as the sounds of the crashing surf filled their ears with the majesty of nature. "This is beautiful, Scott, but I feel very guilty. I should be home working on charity business. It's not just the auction. There's also the fund-raising party afterward and the fund-raising campaign for the upcoming year. There's so much work yet—"

He put his fingertips to her lips, silencing her words. "This weekend is for us." He brushed his lips lightly against hers. "No one is allowed to discuss business."

They went inside and he moved immediately to the fireplace and started a fire. He then uncorked the champagne. With the flames casting soft flickering shadows across the room, they clinked glasses and wordlessly toasted each other. Their eyes locked in an emotional moment that neither could deny. They sipped their champagne and allowed the warm closeness that existed between them to settle around their beings.

After enjoying the quiet time together, they went to the dining room. Dinner was a leisurely affair filled with casual conversation, yet the underlying current of sensuality that flowed swiftly and insistently kept surfacing. The weekend had started on a perfect note. There would be no distractions—nothing to interfere with their enjoyment, nothing to interfere with their quest to learn as much about each other as possible, nothing to interfere with their growing love.

Katherine lay nestled in Scott's arms, her head resting against his shoulder and her hand on his chest. Things were so perfect; she was so happy. She felt his chest rise and fall with the slow even breathing that indicated he had fallen asleep.

A smile curled her mouth as she snuggled closer to him and closed her eyes. They had the entire weekend ahead of them. He would not have to get up in the middle of the night or early in the morning to go home. They would wake up together, as they should. A contented sigh escaped her lips before she, too, slipped into a warm sleep.

Scott remained still. He watched Katherine as she slept in his arms—the gentle rise and fall of her perfectly formed breasts, the loose tendrils of mussed hair resting in disarray against her forehead, her long dark lashes against her cheeks. How exquisitely perfect she was. He could not deny the love he felt for her, the love that welled up inside him whenever he saw her or heard her voice.

She stirred slowly, stretched her legs and wiggled her toes. Her gaze focused on Scott, her voice still thick with sleep. "Good morning. Have you been awake long?" She trailed her fingers across his bare chest.

He brushed the strands of hair away from her face and kissed her forehead. "Not long. I was just relishing the sight of a beautiful naked woman snuggled in my arms." He slid his hand across her stomach, over her hip and up her inner thigh.

She grinned mischievously. "If you're through relishing, then maybe there's something you'd like to do about it?" Her breathing quickened in response to his very tempting touch.

"Mmm...a myriad things come to mind. Everything looks so delicious I don't know where to begin."

"Maybe an invigorating shower would help you make up your mind." She kissed his cheek and flashed him a sly, impish grin before sliding out of bed.

Without saying another word he followed her into the bathroom and turned on the shower, letting it run until the room was warm and steamy. They stepped into the large glass-walled stall together. With water cascading onto his shoulders, he took her in his arms and pulled her against him. Rivulets streamed down their bodies as a thick cloud of steam swirled around their heads. Wet skin clung to wet skin as their passions heated.

His kiss started out soft and gentle, his lips nibbling at the corners of her mouth, his mouth tasting her sweetness. Things quickly escalated as their desire grew. His mouth came down hard against hers—their tongues twining, seeking, exploring. She pressed her body tighter against his; he ran his fingers over the curve of her bottom.

She felt light-headed, lost in the hot swirling cloud of vapor. The shower spray matted her long hair against her neck and several strands stuck to her cheek. She wrapped her leg around his, reveling in the sensation of the hot water running down her body, dripping from her taut nipples, tickling through her dark downy triangle. His hands seemed to be everywhere at once, touching every place he knew excited her.

The intensity of their desire almost overwhelmed her. Her legs felt weak, her heart pounded, she could not catch her breath. Her knees would surely have buckled had it not been for Scott holding her up. Her body was on fire, her nerve endings seared by the heat of passion.

He bent down, lowering his head to capture her nipple in his demanding mouth. He suckled, gently at first, then with an added intensity. When he moved to capture her other nipple she wrapped her arms around his neck and buried her face against his wet hair, her whimpers and moans of delight clearly indicating her heightened state of ecstasy.

His words came out as ragged gasps. ''Oh, Katherine... you're going to be the death of me.'' His legs quivered as he sank to his knees on the floor of the large shower, his hands sliding down her back and his arms wrapped around her hips. He covered her with kisses, his lips nibbling and his tongue tasting as he slowly worked his way down her body, finally arriving at the downy softness between her trembling thighs.

Katherine thought that the only thing preventing her from bursting into flames was the constant spray of water cascading over them. His kisses were hot and demanding; she responded with more ardor than ever before in her life. When his mouth touched the hot core of her pleasure center she threw her head back and allowed the waves of rapture to roll through her body. Her knees buckled as she was no longer able to support her own weight.

She sank to the shower floor, Scott cradling her body to prevent her from being hurt. He smothered her with frenzied kisses, devouring as much of her as he could. He had never before felt the height of arousal that he experienced at that moment. She was his life force, his reason for being.

He pulled her over on top of him as he lay on the shower floor. His strong hands grasped her hips, lifting, then lowering her onto his hardened manhood. His eyes snapped shut as the velvet heat of her femininity tightly encased his arousal. A growl of intense pleasure clawed its way out of his throat as his body stiffened, shuddered, then gave way to hard spasms of rapture.

She felt convulsions overtake her as soon as his heated desire penetrated the very depths of her being. She collapsed forward, falling on top of him. He wrapped his arms around her, holding her tightly in his embrace. The shower spray swept over their bodies, washing their passions away and replacing them with a soft, sensual warmth.

It took several minutes for their breathing to return to normal. Scott wrapped her in the large bath towel and gently patted the water from her skin. He saw the expression on her face, the fires of passion still burning in her eyes. "Don't look at me like that." His voice was soft and teasing. "You've completely zapped all my strength. You wore me out!" He enfolded her in his warm embrace.

She returned his embrace, her voice conveying a shy embarrassment. "I've never made love in a shower before. I didn't know what I was missing."

"We'll have to do it again sometime—sometime real soon." He held her for a long minute before releasing her. "Let's order breakfast from room service. I'm starved!"

Their day was everything she had hoped it would be. After breakfast they rented bicycles and rode down quiet country lanes. That afternoon they walked hand in hand along the nearly deserted beach, pausing to pick up seashells along the way. It was a time of closeness, contentment. They both felt comfortable. Being together felt so right. That night they ate dinner at a small restaurant not too far from the inn where they were staying.

Following dinner they returned to their room. Scott lit a fire in the fireplace and they sat on the floor, watching the flames. Neither spoke; they simply enjoyed being to-

gether. They felt so in tune with each other, so in sync.
Katherine wanted the feeling to last forever.

It was late when they finally went to bed. They made love
slowly and sensuously, rather than with the heated frenzy
that had gripped them that morning. Time had no meaning; they had forever to be together. Every minute of the
day her love for him grew stronger and stronger. They finally succumbed to blissful sleep.

They slept in the next morning. When they woke they
continued to lie in bed, talking softly and savoring the leisurely feeling of not having to get up. Katherine wanted to
tell Scott about her past, share with him her most intimate
and painful secrets, confide things no living person outside of her family and the family attorney knew about, bare
her deepest inner recesses. She wanted to tell him about her
marriage and how much Jeff's callous, uncaring nature had
hurt her—even before his divorce demands for money. She
wanted to tell him about her painful childhood, about the
beatings and her mother's eventual suicide and her own
subsequent feelings of guilt.

She wanted him to know everything. But she hesitated;
for some reason unknown even to herself, she was unable
to tell him. It bothered her that she could not let go of this
last remaining vestige of the ordeal that had haunted her
youth. Perhaps it was because of Jenny. She could not allow herself release from the last remaining hurdle to her
own complete happiness until Jenny was taken care of. She
truly loved the little girl, as much as she loved Scott.

He felt her tremble. "Are you cold?" He put his arms
around her, pulling her to him and sharing the warmth of
his body.

"I guess a little, yes." She snuggled closer to him. A
tremor of apprehension and anxiety shook her body. She
wished she knew how he really felt about her. Did he love
her? Could he possibly love her as much as she loved him?
Her euphoria became tinged with sadness. She hoped he

did not notice. She did not want to spoil what had been a perfect weekend together. She placed a soft kiss on his chest.

He tickled his fingers across her hip, then seductively ran his hand across her bottom. In a voice quickly becoming thick with emotion he whispered in her ear, "If we don't get up and get dressed very soon I'm going to be forced to make love to you again."

"You're turning me into a wanton, brazen woman."

He noted her impish grin and the sparkle in her turquoise eyes. He cupped the fullness of her firm breast, his tongue quickly teasing her nipple to a taut point.

After lunch they packed, then checked out. They drove inland, following the river until they came to a grove of redwoods. After parking the car in a roadside turnout, they walked along the trail, immersing themselves in the sights, sounds and smells of the forest. When they stopped walking the only sounds were the birds, the breeze rustling through the treetops and the occasional cone dropping from a tree branch and hitting the ground with a plopping sound. For a brief moment it seemed to Katherine that they must surely be the only people in the world, isolated from all the ills that have plagued mankind through the ages.

Scott pulled her into his embrace, brushed a loose tendril of hair from her cheek and looked into the depths of her eyes. He placed a soft kiss on her lips.

She slipped her arms around his waist and rested her head against his chest. "Thank you for this weekend. It's been the nicest time I've ever spent anywhere. I hate for it to end."

"Thank you for sharing it with me . . . and it's not over yet. There's one more thing when we get back to town."

She looked at him questioningly. "More? What else could there be? Everything has already been so perfect."

He smiled at her like a little boy with a secret that he was not supposed to tell anyone but was having trouble keeping to himself. "You'll see." He clasped her hand in his and they continued walking.

Scott was beginning to feel the same nervousness he had felt the previous Thursday when he had gone to the jewelry store and picked out the ring. The decision had been very difficult for him. Should he ask her to marry him first, then pick out the ring with her, or should he demonstrate his sincere intentions by already having the ring? He had been very unsure about how to buy a piece of jewelry for someone whose personal wealth was obviously vastly more than his own and who could afford to buy herself the very best.

The whole issue of money frightened him. There were so many unanswered questions. Would she be willing or, for that matter, able to live within the means of his income? Could he adjust to the reality of a wife who was very wealthy in her own right? He had almost turned back at the door of the jewelry store. If he had this many doubts and concerns, then perhaps he was rushing into something.

No. The one thing he did know for sure, the one thing he was positive about, was how much he loved Katherine Fairchild and how much he wanted to spend the rest of his life with her—and that meant marriage, nothing less. He would tell her of his love and ask her to marry him when they got home.

They returned to the car and started back toward San Francisco. It was already late afternoon and they needed to be on the road. As they drove toward town their conversation turned from personal matters to business matters.

"How is Billy doing on his job? I haven't heard anything since the day we were in court, but since I'm responsible for him, I thought I'd better ask."

"He seems to be doing okay. John says he's always on time. Doesn't cause any trouble and does the work assigned to him. In fact, he went one step further. I know it was entirely against his nature to tell on someone, so to speak, but he exposed a situation at the construction site that involved a couple of the crew members who were doing drugs on the job and stealing. Because of him we were able to take care of the matter before it got completely out of hand, and do it in such a manner that no one suspected Billy had any involvement.''

A frown crossed his forehead. ''The only thing that bothers me is why he asked around for a ride to Tiburon each night after work and what he was doing at Mom's house the Saturday we went on our picnic. She said he was helping her with something, but he looked too guilty for it to be that simple.''

Katherine's brow furrowed in thought. ''You know, when I arrived back at the center the day we sent sailing, he was gone and Cheryl didn't know where he was. Lynn was also gone. When she came back she said Billy was running some errands for her.'' She looked quizzically at Scott. ''I wonder what's going on.''

He patted her hand. ''If there was anything wrong I'm sure Mom would have mentioned it.''

They rode along in silence for a little way, then she brightened as if struck by a sudden thought. ''I saw the paperwork on your date package for the auction. Some lucky lady is going to have a very nice weekend. Yosemite Valley is beautiful at that time of year. The big-leaf maples are bright yellow, the oaks have turned golden and the dogwoods are a brilliant red. An added plus is that the park is usually uncrowded, since the summer tourists have gone home and it's too early for snow and skiing.''

''I don't suppose you'd like to bid on me—keep me from being embarrassed when no one wants to bid on me?'' He shot her a mischievous grin.

''I don't think there will be any problem about no one wanting to bid on you. I think the problem will be the bidding war as the ladies fight over you." Her laugh was soft, and her voice showed her amusement at his apprehension. "Anyway, this coming Saturday night will tell us for sure."

"I'm going to feel guilty about running off for the weekend with another woman."

"I'll tell you what—you can make it up to me. The family lodge at Lake Tahoe is available between Christmas and New Year's. We can go there and hide away from the rest of the world...."

It was well after dark when they arrived at Katherine's house. He knew she would be very busy the entire week because of the auction. This would probably be the last time they could spend a significant amount of time alone together. He carried her suitcase up to her bedroom.

"Do you have a schedule showing the sequence of events for the auction?" He set her suitcase on her bed.

"Yes, in my office. There's a file folder in the desk drawer. Why don't you get that and I'll fix us a bite to eat?" She brushed her lips lightly against his and went downstairs. He went into her office and opened the desk drawer.

It had been fifteen minutes and he still had not appeared in the kitchen. She stepped to the bottom of the stairs and called up to him. "Scott? Are you finding what you need?"

Scott descended the stairs, his face a mask except for his silver eyes, which clearly showed the overwhelming emotional pain that flowed through his being. "Yes, *Ms*. Fairchild—I believe I've found everything I need." In his hand was a file folder, the name Scott Blake printed on the tab in large block letters. His voice was totally devoid of any emotion. "In fact, I believe I've found more than you intended, and definitely more than I expected."

Nine

The shock hit her immediately as she recognized the file folder. She had forgotten all about it. She must have accidentally swept it into the drawer with all the others. Panic overtook her. Her stomach churned, her heart pounded, her body trembled. She was barely able to speak. Her throat was dry, her words a whisper. "It's not what you think—"

"No?" He cut her off. "It seems self-explanatory to me. You had me investigated to make sure I was acceptable enough to associate with one of the elite Fairchilds." His voice softened as the hurt welled inside him. "It's a very thorough report. Whoever does your work is quite good— a personal financial statement, a financial statement for the company, my college records, a background check on my parents and an in-depth background check on me. And all this in a report dated only two days after we met."

He flipped open the file to a place that particularly rankled him. "'Numerous affairs handled in a discreet manner, none of them very serious. Applied for a marriage license five years ago, about the time his father died, but never got married. Unknown if there's any connection between the broken engagement and his father's death, or if the two were only coincidental.' You've left no stone unturned. The only thing missing is the number of merit badges I earned when I was a Boy Scout.''

Her eyes brimmed with tears and her body visibly shook. ''Scott, please listen—''

''The games of the rich and famous . . . well, you win the first-place trophy. I fell for it all the way. The only consolation is that things ended before I made a complete fool of myself by doing something—'' his voice cracked as the words choked in his throat ''—like telling you how much I love you and asking you to marry me and share my life.''

He quickly recovered his composure. ''Next time I'll know to stay on my own side of the tracks. The air is too rarified on your side—it prevents me from thinking clearly. Goodbye, *Ms*. Fairchild.'' He dropped the file folder on the table and walked out the door without looking back or pausing. His gut wrenched into a thousand knots.

There had been only one time in his entire life when he had felt as lost and devastated as he did at that moment. It was when his father had suddenly died and his engagement had broken off—both at the same time. He had not thought anything could ever be that bad again. He had been wrong.

He loved Katherine so much more than he had ever loved Carol—there was no comparison. He got in his car and drove home, his mind completely oblivious to anything and everything going on around him.

Scott walked into his bedroom, not bothering to turn on the light, and thrust his hand into his jacket pocket. He withdrew a small velvet box, opened it and removed the exquisite gold-and-diamond ring. His hand closed around the ring, then he clutched it to his heart. He would never love anyone as much as he loved Katherine. He closed his eyes, trying desperately to make the pain go away. He had never known the depth of heartbreak he was experiencing at that moment.

Katherine sank onto a kitchen chair. Her body was numb, her mind was numb, her being was blank. She did not know what to do; she knew only that she wanted to die. How could life be at the very highest peak one minute and crash to the lowest depths fifteen minutes later? She stood up and slowly climbed the stairs to her bedroom. She could never love another man as much as she loved Scott. She collapsed across the bed and cried herself to sleep.

Katherine spent a terrible night, vacillating between utter despair, anger and stubborn determination. After crying until she had no more tears, she began to pull herself together. The despair gave way to the anger.

She was angry at herself for not having destroyed the report immediately, rather than carelessly tossing it on her desk. She was also angry at herself for allowing Scott to leave her house without insisting he listen to an explanation. She was angry at her grandfather for having had Scott investigated in the first place. But mostly she was angry at Scott for not giving her a chance to explain.

His words kept coming back to her, words telling her he loved her and asking her to marry him. She knew in her heart that the words had come from his heart, that they had been his true feelings. She was angry with him for setting aside the love that existed between them and allowing his own injured pride and obstinacy to prevail.

The anger spawned her stubborn determination. She had once told him that she always got what she went after. She would show him just how true that statement was. Katherine loved him more than life itself and she was not going to let that love go by the wayside—she refused to curl up and die.

That may have been what she had wanted to do the night before, but this was a new day and she was fighting mad. Scott Blake had more than met his match. She knew about hurt and rejection. She had learned through painful experience that you do not run and hide—you stand up and fight for what you want. If she did not succeed in getting through to him by Friday afternoon using Plan A, then she would put Plan B into service. One way or the other, she would make him listen to what she had to say.

Scott spoke into the intercom. "Tell Ms. Fairchild that I'm not in. In fact, you can tell her I left the country and you don't know when I'll be back." He glared at the phone. What did she think she was trying to prove by calling him at work? There was nothing left to say—that report had said it all. He had considered canceling out of the auction, but all the publicity was already out and it would not be fair to the charity to leave them in a bind at the last minute. He would just have to make sure he kept clear of her that evening. After Saturday he would put this entire episode behind him and get on with his life.

Time refused to move for Scott; Monday dragged by very slowly. It would seem that hours had passed, but when he glanced at his watch, he would find that it had only been ten minutes. He could not concentrate. Finally he turned off his desk lamp and walked out into Amelia's office. "I'm calling it a day. I'll see you in the morning." He refused to look directly at her, because he knew he would only see her disapproval.

As Scott walked out of Amelia's office into the outside reception area, he spotted Katherine stepping out of the elevator. He quickly turned around and retraced his steps. As he passed Amelia's desk he hurriedly whispered, "I'm not in to Ms. Fairchild. I'll be leaving by my private entrance." He rushed into his office, closing the door behind him.

Katherine walked past the front receptionist and directly into Amelia's office. She tried to project a calm and controlled persona. She extended her most gracious smile as she approached the desk. "Good afternoon, Amelia. I'd like to see Scott. And please don't tell me he's out of the country."

Amelia's gaze traveled nervously around the room, but she was unable to look Katherine in the eye. "He's already gone for the day, Ms. Fairchild."

Katherine looked directly at Amelia. "His car is still in his parking space." She took a seat across the office. "I'll just wait, if you don't mind."

Amelia looked up at her. "You're welcome to wait if you'd like, but he really has gone for the day." Amelia's heart went out to Katherine as she saw the sadness and pain in her eyes.

It had been a lousy week. Scott sank into his chair and swiveled around until he could see out his office window. The low gray clouds threatened rain, the mist obscured the top of the towers on the Golden Gate Bridge, and the wind kicked up whitecaps on the bay. The day was perfect; it fit his mood exactly. He stared blankly out the window, looking but not really seeing.

He turned and opened his desk drawer and withdrew the small velvet box. His intention had been to return it to the jeweler first thing Monday morning. He opened the box and took out the ring. For some reason, some force beyond his conscious control, he had not been able to do so. Perhaps he wanted to keep and savor one small piece of what had been some of the happiest days of his life. He turned the ring over in his fingers, allowing the light to catch the diamonds, causing them to sparkle. He returned the ring to the box and placed the box in his desk drawer.

Amelia entered his office carrying an arrangement of flowers. "Where would you like these? They just arrived."

"From Ms. Fairchild again? How many does that make this week ... ? One a day Monday through Thursday and now two today—six flower arrangements." He sighed heavily. "Do the same thing you did with the others—send them to the hospital. Let someone enjoy them."

"Do you want to read the card?"

"Does it say anything different than the others?"

"No, Mr. Blake. It's the same as the others. 'We have to sit down and talk. Please come to my house at eight o'clock tonight.'"

He knew something needed to be done ... and soon. His state of mind was starting to have an effect on the smooth running of the company. He was forgetting some things and overlooking others. His mind clearly was not on business at all.

As soon as she had concluded the Friday afternoon meeting with the banquet manager at the Hyatt, Katherine stopped by the center and picked up Jenny. She was having an early dinner with her grandfather and wanted to make sure she was home by eight. Her grandfather had specifically requested that she bring the little girl. It warmed her heart to see the way he doted on the child. It was the same type of loving attention he had given her during those dark lonely years of her childhood. It was almost as though Jenny were the great-granddaughter he kept pestering Katherine to provide him with. He had been right; she identified so closely with Jenny and her situation.

She tried to put up a good front, but her distraught condition was more than obvious to her grandfather. There was not, however, an immediate opportunity for him to ask her about it. The little girl had climbed onto his lap and was giggling as she patted his cheek and nose.

Jenny fell asleep on the den couch following dinner. Mincing no words and being as direct as he always had been, R.J. approached his granddaughter. "What's wrong,

Katherine? You look miserable. I know the auction takes a lot of your energy and you're always a basket case the night before because you're sure everything will blow up, but this is different.''

She averted her gaze, not wanting to make eye contact with him. He was capable of getting any secret out of her, including the darkest and deepest secret of her entire life. ''There's nothing wrong, Grandpa. It's like you said—the auction always has me uptight the night before. I'll be fine as soon as it's over.''

His eyes narrowed as he watched the anguish cross her face. ''Katherine Sutton Fairchild, don't you dare lie to me. I can read you like a book.''

She jerked to attention. It had been years since he addressed her by her full name. It was the same manner and tone of voice he had used to persuade her to tell him about her mother and about the beatings. Suddenly she was that frightened little girl again, knowing she could never tell anyone but unable to keep the pain inside any longer. She could not hold back her tears. ''It's Scott, Grandpa.... I love him so much. How could things be so awful?''

In an anguish-filled voice she told him everything that had happened. ''And I know he loves me, Grandpa. I know he does. He's just had his pride hurt and now...'' She could not say any more.

The old man comforted her, a thoughtful look of deep concentration on his face. ''Well, Katherine. It seems I might have a small amount of responsibility in this matter. Perhaps I'd—''

''Don't you dare do anything. It would only make matters worse. I've got to take care of this myself. If you interfere, Scott would just feel as if he was being manipulated even more than he already thinks he has been. Please, Grandpa, don't interfere...promise me!''

''Okay, Katherine. I promise.'' R.J. loved his granddaughter very much. It obviously pained him greatly to see her so upset—and, given the dynamic take-charge type of person he was, his frustration at having his hands tied like that was clearly evident.

Saturday morning found everyone very busy. The auction would begin at seven that night and there were still what seemed like thousands of last-minute details. Everyone's help had been enlisted, and even Billy was lending a hand. By three, things were as ready as they were going to be. Katherine and Liz went over everything on their lists one more time, just to make sure. Lynn double-checked the mailing list and acceptances of the invited guests to the fund-raising party following the auction.

"Could I have everyone's attention?" Katherine's voice rang out loud and clear across the ballroom. "I want to take a few minutes to thank all of you for the hard work you've put in to make this year's auction a rousing success. I think this will be the best one yet." A round of applause greeted her comments.

"There will be the traditional invitation-only after-auction party at my grandfather's, R.J. Fairchild's, house. Make sure you have a printed invitation before leaving this afternoon. They will be collected at the door upon arrival at the party. One more thing—when I start pestering the guests for donations, you're allowed to ignore me." This statement was greeted with laughter.

"You have already contributed more than enough. Again, thank you very much. Now, it's time to go home and put on your finest. We'll meet back here at six. Our bachelors are due at six-thirty, and at seven we'll kick off our fund-raising campaign."

"I ain't so sure about this." Billy caught the disapproving look in Lynn's eye as they walked out the door of the ballroom, headed toward her car. "Yeah, yeah—I know— 'ain't' ain't a word."

"You'll do just fine." She offered him her best confidence-inducing smile.

Scott was having trouble with the black tie. He disliked wearing a tux and really hated wrestling with the tie. On the fourth attempt he finally managed to tie it so that it looked right. He checked his appearance one last time in the full-length mirror.

He picked up the invitation to the party and stared at it. Well, that was one event he certainly had no intention of attending. He stared at it a moment longer and then stuck it in his inside jacket pocket. He decided to bring it along, just in case he got trapped into something. The evening could not be over soon enough to suit him. His stomach was turning flip-flops. The one thing he was dreading most—more than being put on public display, more than this stupid auction idea—was running into Katherine.

His whole being ached; the week had been pure torture. She was everywhere, constantly in his mind. Her sparkling turquoise eyes, her beautiful face, her dazzling smile, her laugh, her body nestled warmly in his arms as she slept. That hauntingly sad expression he had caught just a glimpse of when she had comforted Jenny after the little girl's nightmare, and the emotional words she had said while explaining to Jenny about her mother. Would the love he felt for her ever fade? Would he ever be released from her spell? He closed his eyes and tried to compose himself.

Katherine was a nervous wreck. She had neither seen nor talked to Scott since that horrible moment the previous Sunday when she had allowed him to walk out her door. She had been blessedly thankful for the last-minute frenzied activity surrounding the auction. It had kept her busy, leaving her very little time to reflect on her despair. She had not gotten one good night's sleep for the past week. She knew everyone had been speculating behind her back about what was wrong. She did not know what Lynn knew or suspected, what Scott might have told her.

And there was Jenny—the little girl kept asking where Scott was. She did not know what to tell her. An overwhelming sadness enveloped Katherine. And she did not know if it was for Jenny or for herself. A shudder moved through her body as she turned toward her closet. She needed to hurry or she would be late.

Billy fidgeted as he got out of Lynn's car. It was the first time he had ever worn a suit and tie and it was very awkward and uncomfortable for him. His new shoes felt funny, too. "Jeez, I can't do this."

"You look very nice, Billy. Now, we're going to enjoy the evening's proceedings, then we're going to the party afterward. I think that would be a good time to make our announcement, don't you?"

"Announcement!" Billy's expression suggested that he was into borderline panic. "Come on—I agreed to doin' all this, but—"

"Calm down. You know very well you wouldn't have done it if you hadn't wanted to. All you needed was a little help to get started. You should be very proud of yourself. I'm very proud of you and I know Katherine will be very proud, too. Now, let's go inside."

He eyed her intently for a moment. "What about Scott? Does he know?"

"I promised it would be our secret, that I wouldn't tell anyone what you were doing, and I haven't—not even Scott."

Katherine moved quickly from group to group, talking to everyone for only a few minutes. When she saw Lynn and Billy she immediately rushed to them. "Billy, don't you look nice in your suit and tie. This is a new look for you. Is it something we're going to be seeing more often?"

He gazed at the floor, obviously embarrassed. "Yeah, sort of... yeah. I didn't have nothin'—" He glanced at Lynn, then corrected his grammar. "I didn't have anything proper to wear this evening, so I bought a new suit and this tie." His gaze nervously darted between Lynn and Katherine, seeking their approval. "Is it okay?"

"Yes." Katherine gave him an encouraging smile and a pat on the cheek. "It's perfect." Flashbulbs popped, catching Katherine and Billy together.

Lynn leaned close to Billy and spoke very softly. "Why don't you find our table? I'll be along in just a minute." As soon as Billy was out of earshot Lynn turned her attention to Katherine. "Are you feeling okay? You don't look as though you've been sleeping or eating too well."

Their eyes remained locked for several moments. Lynn could see all manner of emotions flit through Katherine's eyes and across her countenance. She spoke slowly, measuring her words. "I know that whatever is bothering you is none of my business, but if you need a friendly shoulder, I'll be glad to let you use mine. You seemed so happy the past few weeks. You were practically glowing—until this week."

Lynn hesitated a moment before she continued, not wanting to interfere where she was not welcome. "I... I'm aware that you and Scott have been dating. He didn't mention it to me specifically, but it was easy to see. If there's anything you'd like to talk about, I promise to keep it just between you and me."

Katherine gave Lynn a warm hug. "Thank you. Maybe we could..." Her eyes started to mist over and she paused to take a calming breath. "Thank you for your offer. I might take you up on it sometime." She quickly composed herself and went on with the business of greeting people.

Scott stood just inside the door of the ballroom. His throat felt tight and dry. He tried to swallow to lessen the uncomfortable feeling. He had spotted Katherine as soon as he had stepped through the door. His heart skipped a beat and his pulse raced. An unbearable emptiness swept through his being. His stomach knotted. He told himself he should never have gone through with this—seeing her again only heightened his loneliness, his overwhelming need for her.

She was sparkle, she was shine, she was glitter—she was breathtakingly beautiful. Her long beaded gown hugged her curves, the turquoise color an exact match for those incredible eyes he could not get out of his mind. Her smile dazzled everyone she spoke with as she made her way through the growing crowd.

In the same way that a curtain being slowly raised allows the audience to gradually see the entire stage, she became aware of him. She sensed his presence rather than saw or heard him. A lump formed in her throat and her stomach tightened as she turned around, her gaze sweeping across the room until it came to rest on him.

Scott wanted to leave, but his feet refused to move. He felt the panic rise inside his body when her eyes fell on him. He knew it would require very little effort on her part to have him exactly where she wanted him again. He could not allow that to happen.

He wanted to touch her, to hold her, to kiss her—to consume her in a blaze of passion. He wanted things to be the way he had thought they were a week ago, before he had found the proof of how they really were. His body stiffened as he steeled himself against the overpowering temptation of her nearness. He forced himself to hurry across the room and backstage.

Katherine watched him walk quickly away. He could not duck her the entire evening. Their relationship was far from being over. She loved him and she knew he loved her. This stubborn pride of his did more than just make her angry; it spurred her determination. He was not going to get away from her this easily. She had never wanted anyone more than she wanted Scott Blake. No, sir, their relationship was far from being over.

The start of the auction was only minutes away. Liz talked excitedly with Katherine. "This is the biggest crowd we've ever had. I've even heard rumblings of sizable amounts of money—not already-pledged money, but new donations—that are going to be bid." Liz looked around the ballroom at the glittering array of people. "Well, let's get started."

Liz stepped up onstage and the audience quieted immediately. "Good evening, ladies and gentlemen. I'm Liz Torrance. Welcome to our fifth annual charity bachelor auction. If anyone doesn't have a program listing our bachelors and their date packages, please hold up your hand and we'll get one to you." She looked across the crowd. "Okay, it seems that we're all set."

Katherine stood at the back of the room. Liz had things well in hand, as usual. All the bachelors would be introduced and seated on the stage. As their turn came they would step to the podium and give a description of their date package, as briefly outlined in the program, then explain why they had chosen that particular package. She scanned her program. Scott was listed as thirteenth out of fifteen.

The auction progressed smoothly. Everyone was in the spirit of the occasion. Two of the bachelors, a football player and a baseball player, elicited some hefty bids from women who were actually reaching for their own checkbooks.

She had been watching Scott very closely. She was sure no one else could tell, but she could see it in his eyes, in his body language—he would have preferred to be walking barefoot on hot coals through the fires of hell than to be on that stage. A nervous twinge tightened in her stomach. He was up next.

The bidding started immediately and escalated quickly. Four different women were bidding on Scott, two of them volunteer workers bidding money already pledged and two of them bidding their own money. She saw the surprise on his face as the price got higher and higher. The bidding reached the same ten-thousand-dollar level that had bought the football player. Liz asked if there were any more bids as she prepared to close the bidding on Scott.

There was a brief moment of silence, then Katherine's voice carried forward from the back of the ballroom. "Fifteen thousand dollars." Her words were immediately followed by a gasp from the audience and several flashes from photographers' cameras. Liz seemed momentarily startled; Scott was totally stunned.

Liz immediately recovered her composure. "Well, is there anyone who cares to top that?" She looked out over the audience. "No? That's it, then. Sold to Katherine Fairchild for fifteen thousand dollars."

Following the established procedure, Katherine went up onstage to claim her prize. The audience applauded, flash-bulbs popped, videotape cameras recorded everything. She linked her arm with his and maneuvered him offstage to the table reserved for the bachelors and their dates.

She felt his muscles tense as she touched his arm. Tingles of excitement raced through her body as her hand brushed against his. Butterflies flitted around her stomach. This had to work—it just had to. Somehow she had to find some time when they could be alone so she could make him listen to her, make him understand. It might mean telling him everything about her childhood and her marriage—which she had intended to anyway, but not under these circumstances—but if that was what she had to do to make him understand, then that's what she would do.

Scott was furious. It was taking all his effort to remain composed and smile as everyone watched them walk off-stage together. As soon as they were seated he whispered through clenched teeth, "Wasn't it enough for you to make a fool out of me in private without extending your little game to make a fool out of me in public, too?"

She kept her voice low, not wanting to attract any attention to their conversation. "You left me no choice. You kept ignoring my invitation to talk this out."

"There's nothing to talk about."

She continued to speak just above a whisper. "There's a great deal to talk about, and one way or the other you're going to listen to what I have to say."

"You don't seriously expect me to go through with this stupid date thing, do you?" It was more of an angry statement than a question.

Her response was emphatic. "I paid fifteen thousand dollars for the privilege of spending a weekend with you in Yosemite. I expect to get my money's worth."

She saw his jaw tighten as he spoke. "Of course...'your money's worth.'" The tension slackened, his facial muscles relaxed and a hint of despair crept into his voice. "No one asked you to bid on me."

She turned her most dazzling smile on him. "If you recall, you asked me to bid on you just last Sunday."

His response was mumbled and tinged with sadness as he looked away from her. "It was a weak moment of foolishness." The scent of her perfume excited his senses as it wafted across his nostrils. It was the same fragrance she had worn the first time they had met. His skin still tingled where her hand had touched him. He did not understand why she was doing this, what she was trying to prove, what she hoped to gain.

Their conversation was interrupted by the closing of the auction portion of the evening. There was no opportunity for Katherine to have even a few minutes alone with Scott, no chance to explain to him. People were everywhere and they were constantly surrounded. Liz spoke to all the bachelors and their dates, making sure they would all be at the party. There would be press coverage, more publicity photos.

Scott had hoped to slip quietly away without any further involvement. Circumstances, however, dictated that it was not going to happen that way. He would be the object of even more attention and speculation if he did not show up at the party.

The Fairchild mansion was a hubbub of activity. The caterers had everything ready, the valet-parking service awaited the arrival of the guests and it seemed that every light in the house had been turned on. It was definitely one of the gala social events of the year.

Scott pulled his car over to the side of the road a block away from R.J.'s house. He needed a quiet moment to think and to collect himself before entering the glare of the party. He had pretty much been the center of attention following the auction, almost an object of curiosity, because of Katherine's bid. He felt very uncomfortable and awkward knowing his every move and every word were being closely observed.

He was very confused. Try as he might, he could not find any logical reason for Katherine's doing what she was doing. A sigh of despair escaped his lips. He started his car and continued down the street.

"Remember, Grandpa, you promised."

"Katherine, how many times have I told you about this 'Grandpa' business?"

She gave him a quick kiss on the cheek and a teasing smile. "Okay, 'Grandfather.'" Guests had already started arriving. Katherine had hurried from the auction, hoping to have a few words with R.J. before Scott arrived. "I don't know how all of this is going to turn out, but I have to try. I love him and I have to do everything I can to win him back." A tremor moved through her body. "I know he loves me and I want him to come back because of that, not because of anything else.''

Scott turned his car over to the parking attendant and started up the walkway. He paused for a moment and looked around. The place reeked of big-time old-line money. A nervousness jittered through his stomach and a chill ran up his spine. He did not want to be there. He took a calming breath and walked up the steps to the front door. The door opened and the attendant took his invitation.

Katherine was at his side immediately. She seemed to have appeared out of nowhere. She grabbed his hand, tugging insistently. ''Come with me. We're going to talk.''

He removed his hand from her grasp, refusing to follow. ''We have nothing to talk about. I won't be an expendable pawn in whatever this new game is, *Ms*. Fairchild.''

''Scott, please…there is no game and there never was.'' Her voice conveyed every bit of the anguish she felt. ''That file is not what you think—I can explain it. Let's go to a quiet room and—''

''Don't do this to me, Katherine.'' In a voice filled with an aching emptiness he cut off her words. ''Let me heal my wounds so I can get on with my life.''

''Your wounds!'' Her anger flared immediately. ''What about my wounds?''

His anger flared to match hers. ''Why would you have any wounds, *Ms*. Fairchild?'' He quickly glanced around to make sure no one had heard them, then lowered his voice. ''It was your game and you won every round, hands down. You had me all the way. You're the winner.'' His voice became a whisper. ''Now, let me go. I don't want to play anymore.''

Katherine's voice was filled with the same determination that showed on her face. ''We have plenty to talk about and you're going to listen to me—even if I have to tie you to a chair and—''

"There you are, Katherine." Jim Dalton's voice cut into her sentence. "I've a couple of people here you should really meet." He turned a questioning look toward Scott. "You don't mind if I steal her away for a few minutes, do you? I promise she'll be right back."

Scott breathed a sigh of relief. His reserve and determination had started to dissolve the moment he had felt the warmth of her touch when she had grasped his hand. He had been a breath away from agreeing to go anywhere she wanted. "No, I don't mind."

As Jim steered Katherine across the room she turned her head and looked back at Scott. Their eyes met. Their gazes locked for an intense moment, before she was swallowed up by the crowd. He continued to stare at the space she had just vacated. He closed his eyes. The vivid image he held of her danced through his mind.

Ten

"Are you all right, dear?" Lynn placed her hand on Scott's arm. "That's a very strange expression on your face. It would seem to me that any man who just had five women fighting over him to the ultimate tune of fifteen thousand dollars should look happier than you do."

He opened his eyes and quickly collected himself. "Mom, uh..." For the first time he noticed Billy. He was grateful for anything that would allow him to change the conversation. "Billy—a suit and tie?"

"Jeez, why does everyone keep making a big deal out of it?" Billy, obviously embarrassed, put forth an effort to regain control of the situation as he glared at Scott. "What d'ya think, I'm planning on diggin' ditches the rest of my life?"

"Oh? What are your plans?" Scott tried to suppress his amusement at Billy's attempt at being tough in unfamiliar circumstances.

"You can tell John Barclay to look out, I'm after his job. And then—" he leveled a challenging look at Scott "—I think I might like your job. Sittin' in a big office and pushing paper around a desk just might be to my liking."

"Lynn, don't you look lovely this evening!" Jim Dalton had returned, having left Katherine to discuss charity business with some prospective contributors. "There's dancing in the other room. Would you honor me?" He extended his arm to her as he offered a smile that held more than mere courtesy for an acquaintance.

"It's been quite a while since I last danced, but if you promise not to complain if I step on your toes, I would be delighted." She linked her arm with his and they disappeared through the crowd.

Scott watched them with more than idle curiosity. It had been five years since his father's death. His mother was a vibrant, youthful woman. She should be dating, enjoying a social life that consisted of more than her lady friends. Jim Dalton seemed to be a very nice man, a widower himself. Scott approved.

"Looks like your ol'—I mean, looks like Lynn's got a boyfriend." Billy grinned mischievously.

Scott cocked his head and gave Billy an appraising look. "You don't miss much, do you?"

"I see everything, man." Billy looked across the room at Katherine, still busily involved in her conversation, then back at Scott. "I see everything." Scott shifted his weight uncomfortably. "You know, Jenny keeps asking where you are." Having made that pointed comment, Billy abruptly turned and wandered off toward the buffet, leaving Scott standing all alone.

Scott was momentarily lost in thought. Billy's comment about Jenny bothered him. He had missed seeing the little girl, missed her giggle and the way her blond curls bounced up and down, missed the family times they had shared— Katherine, Jenny and him. He was not, however, allowed the solitude of his thoughts for long. A moment later he was swept up in a whirlwind of activity.

Two hours had passed without any opportunity for Katherine to be alone with Scott to talk to him. There were glances across a crowded room, but nothing more. Scott felt confined, closed in. He wanted to leave. Katherine felt frustrated and torn. She needed to be conducting charity fund-raising business, but she desperately wanted to talk to Scott. Too much time had already passed since he had found the file. If this was not resolved soon, she feared it might be too late.

R.J. Fairchild had spent most of the evening with his business associates, making sure they contributed handsomely to the cause. As things began to quiet down, he made his way through the crowd, introducing himself to people he did not know and generally enjoying himself. He had missed the activity and energy associated with big business since his failing health had forced him to step down as chairman of all the Fairchild enterprises three years earlier.

That was why he so enjoyed having Katherine's after-auction fund-raising party at his house. He found it very invigorating. He paused in his purposeful direction toward Scott long enough to speak with Jim Dalton, who introduced him to Lynn.

"It's nice to finally meet you, Lynn. Katherine speaks very highly of you."

Lynn shook hands with R.J., noting the intelligence and curiosity in his eyes. "That's a remarkable granddaughter you have, Mr. Fairchild. I've enjoyed our association very much. Working at the center has been very fulfilling."

"Please, call me R.J. I understand you have a pretty remarkable son, too. I'd like to meet him."

A knot tightened in Scott's stomach as he saw his mother, Jim Dalton and R.J. Fairchild headed his way. He had been able to avoid R.J. for the entire evening; he had thought he was home free.

Lynn introduced them. Scott was surprised at the firmness of the old man's handshake, the strength he possessed. He knew R.J. Fairchild had to be in his eighties and had been confined to a wheelchair due to failing health. However, the man whose hand he had just shaken demonstrated none of those characteristics.

"So you're the young man who has created such a stir. It seems to be all I hear anymore—Scott this, Scott that. Even little Jenny chatters on and on about you." R.J. noted the tenderness that darted through Scott's eyes at the mention of Jenny. "You seem to be everyone's topic of conversation, especially Katherine's." He paused a moment to collect his thoughts, then proceeded cautiously. "I'm probably a little too protective of Katherine—"

"Grandfather!" Katherine's voice abruptly cut into his words. She looked about nervously, her gaze flitting from Jim to Lynn to Scott and finally coming to rest on her grandfather. "You weren't about to divulge any family secrets, were you?" She attempted a teasing smile as she tried to gain control of the conversation.

Scott was immediately struck by Katherine's poorly concealed attempt to hide her nervousness, a nervousness almost bordering on anxiety. It was very out of character for her. He caught the quick look that passed between her and her grandfather. There was definitely more going on than was immediately apparent.

Katherine quickly changed the subject. Spotting Billy across the room, she called him over. "Billy, I'd like you to meet someone. Grandfather, this is Billy Sanchez—you've heard me speak of him."

Billy struck a tough stance as R.J. looked him over then extended his hand. "Hello, young man. It's nice to meet you." Billy shook hands with him. "Katherine has mentioned you on several occasions." Billy shifted uncomfortably from one foot to the other.

Lynn quickly reached out and put her hand on his shoulder, calming his nervousness. "I think now might be a good time for your announcement." She gave him an encouraging smile.

"Yeah, well . . . if you want to tell them, I guess it's okay with me." Billy was obviously embarrassed, just short of blushing.

Lynn turned her attention to include everyone present in their little group. "Ladies and gentlemen, I have an announcement I'd like to make. As of last Thursday evening Mr. Billy Sanchez has passed all the necessary high school equivalency tests for his general education diploma. He's a full-fledged high school graduate."

Billy looked at the floor and mumbled his response. "It's not that big a deal."

Katherine gave him a big hug and a kiss on the cheek. Her enthusiasm was clearly evident. "That's marvelous. I'm so proud of you, Billy."

Jim and R.J. both congratulated him. Scott put his arm around Billy's shoulders and gave him a big smile. "So that's what has been going on with you and Mom. It seems you were very serious when you said you wanted my job. You're off to a good start."

Scott turned toward his mother. "You may be able to take the woman out of the classroom, but you can't take the teacher out of the woman." He gave her a quick wink. "Now tell me, doesn't this beat working in your garden?"

It was late, and the party was rapidly coming to a close. The majority of the guests had gone home. Scott was anxious to leave. He had been trying to leave from the moment fate had intervened to interrupt Katherine's attempts to get him alone. He glanced at his watch. "It's getting late." He directed his comments toward R.J. while extending a gracious smile. "I'm sure you must be tired of all these intruders by now and would like your house back."

"Not at all, young man. I look forward to this gathering every year." R.J. did not want Scott to leave, at least not yet—not until Katherine had had a chance to talk with him.

"I particularly enjoy the time after most of the guests have departed. It gives me an opportunity to have some good conversation with interesting people." R.J. headed his wheelchair toward the garden room as he continued to talk, forcing Scott to follow him. "Now, tell me..."

The next couple of hours passed quickly for Scott. Much to his surprise, he found R.J. easy to talk with and very interesting. He was not at all the dominant imposing figure Scott had anticipated.

Gradually Scott became aware of how quiet the house had become. The sounds of a party had disappeared. He glanced at his watch and was surprised to find that it was after three o'clock. "I had no idea it was so late. I really must be going." He got to his feet and extended his hand toward R.J. "It's been a real pleasure meeting you."

"The pleasure's been all mine. I hope I'll be seeing more of you in the future." It was a very pointed statement, designed to elicit some sort of reaction from Scott. R.J. watched closely. He saw confusion and anxiety cross Scott's face, then quickly disappear as he shifted his weight from one foot to the other, obviously uncomfortable about being put on the spot.

Scott did not know exactly how to respond to R.J.'s statement. It seemed to have been made more emphatically than a mere courtesy dictated. He could feel the panic rising inside him as he realized the full impact of the statement—R.J.'s subtle probing for information. Just how much did he know? How much had Katherine told him? He needed to get away. It suddenly occurred to him that Katherine might be the only one left in the house, that all the guests had gone home. Panic overtook him again. He might not be able to avoid being alone with her.

"I . . . uh . . . really need to be going. I have a long drive back to Tiburon. It's been a pleasure meeting you. Good night, R.J."

"Good night, Scott."

Scott hurried from the garden room, hoping to make it to the front door. He did not see anyone as he made his way through the house. He had almost reached the front door when he spotted Katherine sitting in a chair in a room adjacent to the foyer. She did not see him; her eyes were closed. She appeared to be asleep. He paused a moment to watch her. She seemed so very alone—a little girl lost in a big house. He wanted, with every fiber of his being, to go to her, to put his arms around her, to hold her, to take care of her.

She had been very persistent about wanting to talk to him. Was the fifteen-thousand-dollar bid a desperate attempt to force a discussion, or merely her way of showing him, and everyone else, that he was no more than just another of her many possessions—bought and paid for? As he looked at her now—her shoes on the floor, her legs curled up under her, her head resting on the chair wing—all he could think about was how much he loved her. Scott was very confused; he did not know what to think anymore. Reluctantly, he turned and walked out the front door.

Katherine's phone kept ringing all day Sunday, one call after another, starting at eight o'clock that morning before she was even awake yet. The Sunday newspaper was full of pictures and stories about the auction and fund-raising party. Everyone was very excited. Liz was the first to call. She had been up all night and had just finished tallying the total dollar figure of money raised. Even though she was exhausted, her enthusiasm communicated itself to Katherine. "It's the biggest one to date. We raised over half a million dollars in one evening and pledges are still coming in. The office phone has already started ringing this morning, even though it's Sunday and the offices are supposed to be closed!"

"Half a million? No kidding?" Katherine scooted up into a sitting position in bed, her elation clearly evident as she sat cross-legged and listened to Liz read off some of the major contributions. "Wow! Thirty thousand dollars from Richard Bentley. Grandpa must have really twisted his arm. I think that old tightwad still has the first dollar he ever earned."

"Here's one I think you'll really like. It's a check in the amount of fifty dollars, drawn on a brand-new checking account, from a Mr. Billy Sanchez."

Katherine's eyes misted over as she listened to Liz. Not only had Billy finished high school, worked hard at his job, bought a suit and tie and even opened a checking account, he had actually made a donation to the charity. She was so proud of him.

"You should have seen him, Kat. He was so embarrassed he didn't know what to do. Just before he left R.J.'s house he came over to me, stammered nervously, then shoved the check into my hand and beat it out the door as fast as he could. He was so cute. I called the center this morning to thank him. Cheryl was there. She said he was sound asleep, so I told her not to wake him."

As soon as she finished talking to Liz, Katherine went to the front door and picked up her newspaper from the porch. A frown creased her brow. She was in almost every one of the photos. Once again, the Fairchild name had dominated the newspaper more than the name of the charity or the reason for the event. There was even a picture of her with Billy. She chuckled to herself as she wondered how Billy would explain that to the guys on the construction crew.

The rest of the day went pretty much the same way as the morning, one phone call after another—but no call from Scott.

Scott sat on his couch drinking his morning coffee, even though it was well into the afternoon, and reading the Sunday paper. It had been after four in the morning when he had gotten home, and after sunrise before he had finally gotten to sleep. He had been unable to turn off his thoughts of Katherine and how much he wanted her. Not only did she occupy his conscious thoughts, she dominated his dreams, too.

As he scanned the articles about the auction and the fund-raising party, a new reality hit him. Almost every photo was of Katherine doing something or talking to someone; she was mentioned all the way through every article. But that was not the way it had been at all. Katherine had stayed in the background during the entire auction, except for her one-and-only bid, and had let Liz take charge. It was the same way at the party afterward. She had maintained a low profile and directed the majority of attention to the others who were present.

He put down his paper. Was this typical of the way it had been all along—Katherine trying to stay out of the center of publicity but her name making it impossible for her to do so? That was certainly the way he had perceived it last night. The newspaper account did not give an accurate portrayal at all. He reflected on her moment of sad resignation when he had asked her how she put up with always being in the public eye, and her only response had been that one eventually got used to it. Perhaps the fifteen-thousand-dollar bid really was... He felt a glimmer of hope start to break though his despair.

Scott pulled his car into the circular drive at his mother's house. He knew he probably should have called first, but instead he had impulsively driven over. It had been quite a while since they had shared Sunday evening dinner at the little Sausalito restaurant that had been a family favorite when he was growing up. His mind was too full of thoughts of Katherine and Jenny, of how he missed the times they had shared. He desperately wanted, actually needed, to recapture that feeling of family closeness.

"I'm afraid I'm not quite ready...." Lynn's words trailed off as she realized it was Scott standing on the other side of her door. "Scott, dear. What are you doing here?" Her surprise was clearly evident.

He offered her a teasing grin. "Is that any way to greet your favorite son?" The grin faded as he noticed the way she was dressed. She had not been lounging around the house; she was dressed to go out. "Am I interrupting something? Those aren't exactly your 'working in the garden' clothes."

"Of course you're not interrupting. Don't stand out there on the porch—come in."

He closed the door after entering the house. "I thought we might go to Sausalito for Sunday night dinner, if you're not busy. We haven't done that for quite a while."

"Well, actually...I do have a dinner engagement for this evening."

He lifted his eyebrows as he cocked his head. "Really? With whom?" Suddenly the realization hit him. The sly, knowing grin slowly spread across his face. "You have a date with Jim Dalton." He saw the blush cover his mother's cheeks as she lowered her eyes.

"It's not really a 'date.' Dating is for young people, like you and Katherine. We're simply having dinner together, that's all."

The look of despair that flashed across his face and through his eyes at the mention of Katherine was unmistakable. Lynn cautiously ventured forth, now that the subject had been raised. "What's wrong, dear? You've seemed quite out of sorts lately. Are you and Katherine having problems?''

He tried to cover his inner turmoil. ''There's nothing wrong...'' He could not finish his sentence; his voice just trailed off.

She leveled a stern look at him. ''You know I try never to interfere in your personal life. There's nothing worse than a grown man who has a mother who's always meddling in his life as though he were still a little boy.'' She saw the wariness come into his eyes. ''But I have something to say, and I want you to listen.''

Lynn sat on the couch and motioned for him to join her. ''You know I loved your father very much. He was the kindest, most caring man I ever knew. He was also the most stubborn. Well, my favorite son, I believe you've surpassed him in the stubborn department.''

Scott looked at her, clearly shocked by her words, his voice very defensive. ''What are you talking about?''

''I'm talking about you and Katherine. The poor girl is obviously distraught and you're a mess. I don't know what's going on or what has happened, but I'm sure your stubborn attitude is not helping.''

She gave him a loving pat on the cheek, then stood up. ''That's all I'm going to say on the subject. Now, I have an engage...'' She gave him an impish grin. ''I have a 'date' and I'm not ready yet, so I'll have to ask you to run along.'' Without further ado, she ushered a startled Scott out her front door just as Jim Dalton pulled into the driveway.

''Give me a beer, Terry.'' Scott slid onto the end bar stool at the waterfront pub just a couple of blocks from his house. He grabbed a handful of peanuts and absentmindedly tossed a couple of them in his mouth as he stared out the window at the ocean.

The bartender poured a draft beer and set it in front of him. ''Here you go, Scott.'' He paused a moment, but Scott did not respond, just kept staring blankly out the window. He waved his hand in front of Scott's face. "Hey, Earth to Scott, Earth to Scott...."

"Huh? Oh, sorry, Terry. I've got a lot on my mind." He picked up the glass of beer and took a sip.

"Hi, Scott." The sultry voice of Susan, the cocktail waitress, drifted over him as she slipped her arm around his shoulders. "It's been a while since we've seen you. Where have you been keeping yourself?"

He ignored her obvious attempts to flirt with him. "I've been busy lately, a new construction project."

Terry laughed an open, outgoing laugh. "That's not all you've been busy with, if this morning's paper is anything to judge by. That was quite some picture of you and the famous Katherine Fairchild."

A look of intense irritation crossed Scott's face. "Cut it out, Terry. It was a charity thing, that's all."

"Tell me, Scott..." Susan brushed her body against his, being anything but subtle. "Exactly what makes you worth fifteen thousand dollars?"

He stared at her without really seeing her. A horde of thoughts raced through his mind. What did make him worth fifteen thousand dollars? Certainly not just proving a point or playing a game. He reached into his pocket and put some money on the bar. "Here's for the beer." He rose from the bar stool and headed for the door. "See ya later." Scott left the bar, leaving a very perplexed Terry and Susan staring after him.

He walked home, the brisk evening air soothing his confusion. His mother's words played through his mind; the image of Katherine curled up in the chair by the front door of R.J.'s house kept popping into his consciousness; his overwhelming love for her filled his being. He had thought he had everything figured out, but now he no longer knew what was real and what was not.

* * *

The nonstop phone calls finally came to an end and Katherine was able to sit back and relax. She felt drained, both physically and emotionally. The auction had worn her out, but the added strain of her emotional turmoil had left her exhausted. Several times during the day she had reached for the phone to call Scott. Sometimes an incoming call made that impossible, other times she would pause, then withdraw her hand.

She had been most unhappy with herself for falling asleep in the chair by the door. When her grandfather had woken her and told her Scott had already left, her heart had sunk in despair. She felt it had been her last chance to get him alone. She knew R.J. had done his best to keep Scott occupied until all the guests had departed, but she had blown it. She had just been too tired to keep her eyes open any longer. A shiver shook her body as a sob caught in her throat.

She lay in bed staring at the ceiling, wondering what the future would bring, wondering if she could go on without Scott. *Katherine Sutton Fairchild, listen to yourself. You sound like a quitter.* A look of determination crossed her face. *Fate doesn't just happen—you make it happen. I may have missed this opportunity, but I'll see to it that there's another one. This is not over, and it won't be over until Scott has his arms wrapped around me and is telling me how much he loves me. One way or the other, that's the way it's going to be.*

Katherine pounded her pillow into a comfortable shape, turned over and closed her eyes.

Scott, too, lay in bed staring at the ceiling, his mind trying to put some organization to his confused thoughts. The one thing he knew for sure was that the past week had been the most miserable of his life. He finally fell into a restless sleep, bits and pieces of dreams running through his subconscious, snatches of information trying to connect into some sort of reality.

Scott awoke with a start. It was already daylight. The sheets and covers were a tangled mess; he had obviously tossed and turned all night. He did have one very clear, crystallized thought in his head: he had been wrong to ignore Katherine's attempts to talk to him, to refuse to listen to her. His mother had been right—he was a stubborn damn fool. Maybe those had not been her exact words, but he knew that was exactly what she meant.

He took a quick shower, dressed and went to the phone. With a slightly trembling hand he dialed Katherine's number. The phone rang several times, but no one answered, not even her answering machine. He replaced the receiver in the cradle.

Katherine was under the shower, rinsing the shampoo from her hair, when she thought she heard the phone ringing. She turned off the water and listened, but heard nothing. She quickly finished, dried her hair, dressed and dashed out the door. She was late for a breakfast meeting.

After the meeting she stopped by the florist and picked out a flower arrangement. She paused as she thought about the message she wanted to write on the card.

The next item on her agenda was shopping. It was Halloween and she would be taking Jenny trick-or-treating that evening. She was looking forward to sharing Jenny's first costume and first trick or treat. A moment of sadness came over her. There was only one thing missing that kept everything from being perfect—Scott.

She smiled to herself as she visualized the little girl's excitement earlier, how her face had glowed as she had talked about being a fairy princess with a crown and a magic wand. Then the warm glow faded as she remembered what else Jenny had wanted—she wanted Scott to go with them. Katherine had not known what to tell Jenny, so she said that he was very busy with work and did not think he would be able to go. Her heart had ached when she had seen the look of disappointment on Jenny's face.

Scott drove directly to the construction site in San Rafael before going to the office. He'd had a progress meeting with John Barclay in the office trailer, then taken a look around the site. Things were coming along nicely, and right on schedule.

The crew was on a morning coffee break. He noticed a group of men gathered around Billy, one of them holding Sunday's newspaper. As he passed them he heard Billy saying, "Yeah, me and Kat go back a long way." Billy was clearly enjoying his new celebrity status.

As soon as he arrived at his office he tried calling Katherine again. There was still no answer. She must have forgotten to turn on her answering machine. He called two more times that morning, then tried her at the charity's offices. They had not seen her. He called the Oakland center. He heard the cool reserve in Cheryl's voice when she told him Katherine was not there.

Shortly after lunch Amelia walked into his office carrying an arrangement of flowers. Her irritation was clearly apparent. "Mr. Blake, this is the last straw. Please do something about this." She handed him the sealed envelope containing the card that accompanied the flowers.

"I think those flowers would look nice in your office." He smiled as he took the envelope from her.

This new attitude on his part was surprising. Amelia hesitated for a moment, her brow wrinkling, then turned and carried the flowers to her office, tactfully closing the office door behind her.

Scott's heart pounded. Katherine was still trying to get in touch with him. She had not written him off, even though she certainly had every right to do just that. With trembling fingers he removed the card from the envelope:

"I'm taking Jenny trick-or-treating this evening. Please come." He held the card in his hand and read it a second time. Yes, he would like that very much. A warm feeling of happiness settled inside him, the first calm moment he had felt since that terrible Sunday night.

He glanced at his watch. Scott needed to find himself a Halloween costume. He headed for the door, then paused and returned to his desk. He opened the drawer and removed the small velvet box.

Eleven

———

Katherine swung by the Oakland center to pick up Jenny.
She did not see Cheryl and did not have time to wait for her
to return. She wanted to get home before the evening rush-
hour traffic piled up.

Her grandfather had promised to come to her house to
have an early dinner with them. He had even agreed to stay
the evening and hand out candy to the children who came
to the door while she was out with Jenny. She chuckled to
herself. She wondered what the board members of the numerous Fairchild enterprises would say if they knew R.J.
Fairchild was personally handing out trick-or-treat candy.

Her grandfather had taken her trick-or-treating every
Halloween from the time she was a little girl, even before
her mother... Katherine glanced toward Jenny, strapped
securely into the car seat. *I promise you, I'll see to it that
you're never denied the joys and pleasures due all children
as they grow up—that you'll always have someone who*

loves you. She reached out and touched the little girl's blond curls.

Jenny turned her attention to Katherine. "Will Scott be there?" Her big brown eyes were filled with innocence and questions.

"I don't know, precious. He...he said he'd try." She saw the disappointment in the child's eyes. She quickly turned her attention back to the road.

Jenny was so excited she could hardly stand still. She kept jumping up and down and clapping her hands as Katherine tried to get her into her costume. Dinner had already been prepared, and only needed to be heated when R.J. arrived. Jenny and Katherine both heard the car as it pulled up in front of the house. The little girl ran from Katherine's bedroom and down the stairs. "Scott... Scott..."

"Jenny, wait a minute. Don't go so fast, you'll hurt yourself." Katherine went after her, surprised at how quickly the child had slipped out of her reach.

Scott had been in and out of every costume shop in San Francisco. Every one was sold out of anything and everything even remotely close to his size. Finally he settled on just a mask. The hour was getting late and he wanted to make sure he got to Katherine's house before they left on their rounds. He had tried several times, unsuccessfully, to reach her by phone to tell her he would be there.

He pulled up to Katherine's house and parked at the curb. A shiver of panic cut through him when he saw the limo in the driveway and the police car at the curb. He quickly went to the door and rang the bell, then knocked.

"R.J.!" Even though he instinctively knew the limo belonged to R.J., he was still surprised to see him opening the front door. Then a deep fear spread through him as he saw the two police officers standing on the other side of the living room, engaged in very serious conversation. One of the officers left, excusing himself as he pushed by Scott and out the front door.

Tremors of fear shook his stomach as he entered the house. In a voice barely above a whisper he managed to force out some words. "What's going on . . . ? Katherine . . . is she . . . ?"

"Katherine is fine. She's in her bedroom." Scott immediately turned toward the stairs, but R.J. stopped him. "One moment, young man." R.J. propelled his wheelchair to where Scott stood at the foot of the staircase.

"Katherine is fine physically. Emotionally, it's a different story. Jenny is missing." He noted the look of anxiety that quickly covered Scott's face. "She heard a car pull up in front of the house and thought it was you. She got away from Katherine and was out the door before Katherine could stop her. She simply disappeared into the darkness. Katherine spent half an hour looking for her, then called the police."

"Why would Jenny have thought it was me?" As soon as the words were out of his mouth he realized how stupid they sounded. He did not even know why he had said them.

"Because she has been asking for you all week, kept asking Katherine if you were going trick-or-treating with them." R.J. leveled a cool look at Scott. He could see how distraught Scott was but still found his question odd. "Katherine didn't know what to say. She didn't want to tell the little girl yes and then have her be disappointed and hurt when you didn't show up."

The pain stabbed deep inside Scott as he listened to what R.J. was saying. His own misery of the past week had blocked out any and all consideration of what anyone else was going through. He had selfishly wallowed in his own self-pity without a hint of consideration for anyone else. Again he turned toward the stairs. His voice was very soft and clearly conveyed all the emotions coursing through his being. "I have to go to Katherine. She must be terribly upset about Jenny... and very angry with me."

"Before you go up there..." R.J. reached out and actually grabbed Scott's arm to halt him. "I want to tell you a story—a story about a little girl."

A hint of irritation crept into Scott's voice. He did not have time for this; he wanted to get to Katherine, comfort her and ask her forgiveness—beg for it if that was what it took. He touched the small velvet box in his jacket pocket, and wanted to tell her how much he loved her. "I know all about Jenny's background."

"I'm not talking about Jenny." He gave Scott a stern look, carefully weighing his words as he balanced his promise to Katherine against the necessity of the moment. "I want to tell you a story about a little girl who everyone thought had everything a little girl could possibly want. Now, mind you, this is just a story. Interpret it however you like."

Scott stood in the dimness of Katherine's bedroom, the only light coming from a small table lamp next to the bed. She stood on the deck staring out into the darkness, her arms crossed as she hugged her shoulders against the damp cold. She looked so fragile, so in need of someone to take care of her. He watched her for a moment.

Katherine felt numb inside. The tears trickled down her cheeks. How could she have been so careless as to let Jenny slip out the door like that? *If anything happens to her...I'll never be able to forgive myself.*

"Katherine?"

The soft voice coming from directly behind her startled her. She had not been aware of anyone entering the room. She slowly turned around until she faced Scott. At first she did not know what to do, so she just stood there, the cold damp air covering her like a blanket. Finally she spoke, her voice quivering with emotion. "She's all alone out there, so lost and alone."

Scott saw the agony and fear in her tear-streaked face. His heart ached as he responded to her words. "Kind of like you?"

She stared at him, not comprehending what he was saying. Then the light of recognition came into her eyes. Her gaze dropped to the floor.

He walked to her side, placed his fingertips under her chin and raised her face until he could see into her eyes. "I've behaved like a first-rate jackass and a damned fool."

Katherine did not know what she felt. Her despair over Jenny had left her benumbed, yet the sight of Scott and the sound of his voice warmed her, easing that despair. She let herself be folded in the security of his embrace. She did not have the energy to engage in any verbal jousting. She was just thankful that he was there. She said the first thing that came to her mind. "That's absolutely correct—you've been behaving like a real jackass."

Her words were true and said without any hint of anger or recrimination. He smiled at her honesty. "I see we've found an area of agreement. Can you ever forgive me?"

She shuddered as an intense emotion washed over her being. She tried her best to hold back the sobs. "He told you, didn't he? He promised me he wouldn't. I wanted you to come back because you wanted to, not because you felt sorry for me—'poor little rich girl' and all that."

His voice was barely above a whisper. "All he told me was a story, only a story." He pulled her closer to him, holding her tighter as he caressed her back and twined his fingers in her hair. He felt her soft warmth as she rested her head against his shoulder. His heart beat faster as his own emotional state washed over his being. "Please forgive me, Katherine. More than anything I want to erase this past week. It's been the most horrible week of my life. That file doesn't matter. What does matter is that we're together."

He took a steadying breath. Even though the circumstances were wrong, he had to tell her he loved her and he had to tell her now. He lowered his head and lightly brushed his lips against hers. He held her head to his shoulder and rested his cheek against her hair. "I love you, Katherine. I love you very much. I don't want us to ever be apart again."

His words sent a euphoria through her being unlike anything she had ever experienced. She sent up a silent prayer: *Please let it be true.* "Oh, Scott. I can't even describe how much I love you. I've loved you from the first moment we shook hands in your office."

Scott trembled with elation; her words were music to his ears. "Then you're a little quicker than I am. I don't think I fell in love with you until a couple of hours later, in the elevator of the Hyatt." He continued to hold her, stroke her hair, caress her shoulders.

The shared moment when they confessed their love for each other was unusually subdued, given the nature of their words. Both were torn between two extremes—the overwhelming joy of their love and the very real anxiety of the lost Jenny. What should have been a moment of unbridled rhapsody was, instead, one tinged with an increasing sense of panic as the hour grew later and later.

Katherine and Scott sat on the couch in her bedroom, his arm protectively around her shoulders as he held her to him. The doorbell had been ringing all evening. Each time she heard it she jumped to her feet, but it was always the same—only children trick-or-treating. R.J. stayed downstairs and took care of the candy chores, shooing Katherine and Scott back upstairs.

She raised her head from his shoulder and looked into his eyes. "It's been over two hours. Where could she be?"

He brushed his lips gently against hers. "I'm sure she's okay. Try not to worry." A frown wrinkled his brow. He wished he believed his own words. He felt her sigh of despair as the doorbell rang again.

"Oh, Scott... I don't know what I'll do if anything happens to her." A shudder moved through her as she tried to suppress the sobs, and the tears welled in her eyes. She clung to him, needing and taking the strength and comfort he provided her.

A sound, some sort of mechanical noise, caught his attention. He did not recall ever having heard it in Katherine's house. Then, at the head of the stairs, a sliding door opened. R.J. emerged from the small elevator. Sitting in his lap was an adorable little girl dressed as a fairy princess. Jenny giggled as R.J. pushed the lever to guide the wheelchair across the room.

Katherine's eyes had been closed while she leaned against Scott. He quickly moved her upright, his heart beating with his excitement. "Katherine—look."

"Jenny!" Katherine jumped up from the couch and ran across the room. She snatched the little girl away from R.J., wrapping her arms around the giggling child. She hugged Jenny tightly against her body, tears of relief and happiness streaming down her cheeks. "Are you all right, my little precious?"

She turned toward R.J. as she continued to hold Jenny to her. "Where did they find her?"

"According to the police officer who brought her back, she joined a group of children who were trick-or-treating, went from house to house with them. The mother who was accompanying the kids didn't realize she had an extra one until an hour later. She tried to find out who Jenny was and where she lived, but the only thing she could learn was that she had been 'at Kat's house,' which made no sense to the woman, so she called the police."

"She seems to be okay."

"She's just fine. The policeman said she was having a grand old time."

Katherine felt Scott's arm slip around her shoulders, felt the warmth of his touch. She covered his hand with hers, relishing the sensation of his closeness.

"Scott... Scott." Jenny wiggled in Katherine's arms as she tried to reach him, her blond curls bouncing up and down with her excitement. "We went to one house that had a witch. Everybody was scared except me. Another house had a ghost, but it wasn't really a ghost. It was just a man dressed up like a ghost."

He took the giggling little girl from Katherine's arms. Jenny's tiny hand patted Scott on the cheek, then she wrapped her arms around his neck.

"Well," R.J. interjected, "it looks like you don't need me here. I'll go back downstairs and tend to the candy duty." With that, he propelled his wheelchair toward the elevator.

"Jenny, precious, I was so worried about you. You shouldn't run off like that. You could have been hurt. Scott came to go trick-or-treating with us. He's been very worried about you, too."

"That's right, Jenny." Scott touched the little girl's cheek in a loving gesture. "We've all been very worried."

Jenny yawned as she snuggled in Scott's arms. She had been involved in a very big adventure for a three-year-old and was exhausted. Scott carried her downstairs to the guest room. Katherine folded back the covers, then Scott laid Jenny in the bed. Katherine removed Jenny's shoes. The little girl was still wearing her costume. She was sound asleep. Katherine covered her with the blanket and kissed her on the cheek. "Good night, Jenny."

Katherine and Scott watched as Jenny slept peacefully in the big bed, seemingly without a care in the world. They were both lost in their own thoughts. Scott turned out the light and he and Katherine went back upstairs, his arm around her shoulders and her arm around his waist. They were greatly relieved that Jenny had been found and was unharmed—not only unharmed but apparently delighted with her adventure.

They sat on the couch, and Scott drew Katherine to him, his arms holding her in a warm embrace. He ran his fingertips across her cheek as he spoke in a soft, loving voice. "She didn't seem to be upset or frightened. I think she's just fine."

"I hope so." Katherine's voice reflected the emotional strain she had been under; now that the crisis was over she could give in to her exhaustion. She stifled a yawn.

Scott kissed her on the cheek. "You're tired. Perhaps I should go home for now. We can have dinner together tomorrow night."

She looked searchingly into his eyes. "How do I know you'll come back?"

He saw her anxiety, felt her concern. "Katherine... please Katherine." His arms tightened around her as his own emotions took hold. "Please forgive me. I love you so very much." He lowered his head and brushed his lips softly against hers before capturing her mouth in a loving kiss.

Her fingers trembled slightly as she touched them to his cheek. She felt the heat of his passion. Even though his kiss was soft the meaning was very deep. "No, don't go. Grandpa will be leaving in a little while and we can be alone, have time to get to know each other again."

His voice was a verbal caress. "I'd like that... very much." He felt such an inner calm just being able to hold her in his embrace.

"Let's go to the den. You can build a nice fire in the fireplace and I'll see how the candy supply is holding out. I would imagine most of the trick-or-treaters have already made the rounds."

Scott paused at the door of the guest room to check on Jenny as Katherine continued on down the stairs. The little girl was still sleeping peacefully. He went across the hall to the den and started a fire.

Downstairs, Katherine walked to where her grandfather had positioned himself by the front door. "Grandpa, how are you doing?"

"I was just about to come and get you. Things are pretty quiet now. I think I can close up shop and have James drive me home." He glanced toward the stairs, making sure he and Katherine were alone. He leaned toward her and spoke in a quiet voice. "How are things with you and Scott? It's the way you wanted it to be, isn't it? He did come here on his own."

She tried to give him a stern look but was not able to hold it. "I don't know what to do with you, Grandpa. You promised me you wouldn't interfere and then you turned around and told him about..." Her voice trailed off. He may have come to her house on his own, but was he staying because he really loved her or...?

"Katherine, I know you sometimes think I'm a meddling old fool, but you know how much I love you. I only want your happiness—you deserve it."

"I know, Grandpa. I know." She leaned over and kissed him on the cheek, then brought him his coat. The chauffeur helped R.J. to his limo. She closed and locked the front door, turning out the porch light, then hurried back to the den and to Scott.

Scott was seated on the floor among the large pillows. He had poured Katherine and himself a glass of wine. As he heard her coming up the stairs, he reached to where his jacket rested on the arm of the love seat and touched the pocket, reassuring himself that the small velvet box was still there. He felt nervous. She had never said she forgave him. She had told him she loved him and had asked him to stay but had not told him that she forgave him for his terrible behavior of the previous week.

Katherine paused at the den door. Only the light from the flames lit the room, casting soft shadows on the walls and flickering highlights on his handsome features. He had a worried, pensive look on his face as he stared into the flames. She loved him so much. She hoped they would be able to put the previous week behind them and get on with their lives, what she hoped would be their lives together.

"I see you've poured us each a glass of wine. A little trick-or-treat goody for us adults?" She flashed him a dazzling smile.

"No tricks, only a treat" was his teasing reply. He returned her smile. "Come here and sit down. You look lonely over there all by yourself."

She quickly moved to sit beside him on the large floor pillows. He handed her the glass of wine, allowing his fingers to touch the soft warmth of her hand. He held up his glass toward her, then clinked it against hers. "To you." He looked intently and lovingly into the depths of her eyes. "I love you, Katherine. I love you very much."

His voice cracked as his words choked in his throat, the emotion almost too much for him. "I'm sorry, Katherine. I'm so sorry for everything I've put you through. I don't deserve your forgiveness, but please tell me you forgive me anyway. I have to hear you say the words. I have to know that it's true."

She looked at him for a long moment. She saw the anxiety in his eyes. Slowly she leaned forward and brushed her lips softly against his. Her words were whispered. "I love you. Of course I forgive you—this time. But don't ever do that to me again. I don't think I could live through it a second time."

He set down his wineglass and enfolded her in his arms, reveling in her closeness. He murmured the words in her ear. "What do you want? What do you want the future to be? What can I do that will make you happy?"

She felt a tremor move through her. What was he asking? What was really on his mind? What she wanted more than anything was a home with Scott and Jenny—she wanted them to be a family. Was she wanting too much? Her words were tentative, hesitant. "I... I don't know." She looked questioningly into his eyes, searching for answers. "What are you willing to give? How much of a commitment are you ready to make?"

How much of a commitment was he willing to make? That was an easy question. He had purchased his proof of commitment before they had gone away for the weekend. Now was the time to share it with her. "I think I have an answer to your question right here in my jacket pocket." He withdrew the small box and turned back toward her.

Katherine's eyes grew wide with surprise as she saw the small velvet box. Her heart beat faster and her pulse raced. Did she dare to hope that it was what she thought it was? She was almost afraid to breathe. She watched as he opened the box, the tension in the air almost too much for her to handle.

The diamonds captured and reflected the light from the flames as the ring sparkled against the black velvet background. He withdrew it from the box and then took her hand in his. With trembling hands he slipped the exquisite ring on her finger. "Marry me, Katherine. I want to spend the rest of my life with you."

Tears of happiness welled in her eyes as she looked at the ring on her finger. Shivers shook her body. Her hand trembled. Her voice quavered. "Are you really sure? Do you really want to marry me?"

"Do I want to marry you?" He cupped her face in his hands and kissed her lovingly and deeply. Every bit of emotion and tender care that he felt for her were clearly conveyed through every fiber of his being. "More than anything in the world I want to marry you."

Before she answered him she wanted to bring every possible doubt and concern that he might be harboring deep inside himself out into the open. "It doesn't matter that I'm rich and can afford to buy anything and everything I want? It doesn't matter that everywhere I go someone from the press takes my picture? It doesn't matter that I seem always to be in the glare of the public eye?"

He felt her tremble in his arms as she continued to speak. The questions she was asking him had been the same ones he had asked himself, more than once. "Nothing matters other than our being together. I love you, Katherine."

She took a steadying breath, her insides trembling with anxiety. "You say it doesn't matter now—but what happens a year from now?" She looked into his eyes, all the fear and panic that churned inside her clearly showing. "What about five years from now, Scott? What happens then?" A sob caught in her throat. She feared the reality of his answer.

"As long as we love each other everything else can be managed, and I know for a fact that there's nothing that can outweigh the love I feel for you."

"I've watched you—watched you at the press conference and at the auction. It was very obvious how uncomfortable you felt being in the spotlight. What happens when…?" The panic rose up inside her almost to the point of choking off her words entirely. "What happens when someone calls you 'Mr. Fairchild' rather than referring to me as 'Mrs. Blake'? Will you be able to manage that?"

Scott felt the first very real tremors of total panic. His voice trembled as he spoke. "Katherine, you're scaring me. What are you trying to tell me?"

"I'm only trying to bring the obvious problems out in the open, problems that will be unique to our situation."

Full-blown panic gripped his insides. He wrapped his arms tightly around her. "I love you more than I'm capable of telling you. I know there will be problems that we'll have to overcome, unique problems. We can work them out together. Our love will allow us to handle whatever comes along. Marry me, Katherine.''

Her mouth was so close to his that their lips brushed together as she whispered, "What about Jenny?"

George Weddington unrolled the plans on top of the table in Scott's office. "I've incorporated all the changes you asked for. Does this look like what you had in mind?"

Scott studied the blueprints, noting the changes from the original plans. "The more I think about it, the more I feel we should extend this wall out another five feet and add the other room we discussed. If we put it here—" he indicated the place on the blueprints "—we can do it without disturbing that large old oak tree."

George sighed as he rolled up the plans. "If you don't stop changing things, you'll never be able to start construction. I can see it now—we'll be into the next century and you'll still be moving walls and changing windows." He gave Scott a warm smile. "I'll make the changes this afternoon."

"I promise, this will be it—honest." The two men shook hands and George departed Scott's office.

Scott leaned back in his chair and swiveled around until he could look out the window. The past two weeks had been the busiest of his life, too many projects and too little time. The weather had been unseasonably warm and dry, and he hoped it held for a while longer. He did not want bad weather to delay completion of his primary construction project. He glanced at his watch. He needed to be on his way. He had a meeting at the attorney's office, then that most important of meetings immediately afterward—a meeting with the state's child-welfare agency.

Twelve

The snow blanketed the surrounding mountains with a pristine cover of soft white, accentuating the brilliant blue waters of Lake Tahoe. The branches of the pine trees drooped low as the clumps of snow adhered to the pine needles. Large wet flakes floated by the windows as they gently fell from the skies. The scene looked as though it had been taken directly off the front of a Christmas card. A roaring fire danced and crackled in the large stone fireplace. Two pairs of skis and two sets of ski poles were propped up in the corner, and two pairs of ski boots rested on the floor.

Scott filled Katherine's cup with hot spiced cider, laced with a noticeable amount of brandy, then filled his own cup. They sat on the floor, warming themselves in front of the fire. He leaned close to her, brushed his lips against hers, then spoke. "Are you sure you don't want me to try for some dinner reservations for tonight?"

Her laugh was soft as she stroked his cheek with her fingertips and returned his soft kiss. "You can't wait until the afternoon of December 31 to start thinking about dinner reservations for New Year's Eve. Besides, I'd rather spend the evening away from all those crowds of people." She snuggled in his arms. "I'd rather spend the evening right here, just the two of us."

He kissed her cheek. "Me, too." He furrowed his brow in thought for a moment. "How long can we stay here—I mean, just the two of us, before some of your family show up?"

"Day after tomorrow Uncle Charlie and Aunt Rose will be here, and by the end of the week their whole family will be here, kids and all."

"Ouch! Then we need to be out of here after New Year's Day, or be inundated with your relatives."

She laughed at the scrunched-up expression on his face. "That's not polite, but it's definitely accurate."

He turned her around in his arms until she faced him. His gaze moved over her face, then settled on her eyes. "I love you so much. You're my life, my reason for being." He lowered his head to hers, capturing her mouth in a loving kiss.

She returned his kiss, conveying all the deep feelings she held for him. "I never knew it was possible to love someone as much as I love you."

He cupped her face in his hands, his expression very serious. "I know we discussed it and I know I agreed with you, but I can't wait any longer." He rose to his feet, pulling her up with him. "Right now!"

"Now?"

"Yes, right now." He pulled her along behind him as he walked across the room.

* * *

"Do you, Katherine Sutton Fairchild, take this man...?"
Scott clasped her hand tightly in his as the minister began
the ceremony. The small wedding chapel, located at the
water's edge, was only a few blocks from the Fairchild
family lodge.

They had discussed the wedding several times. Neither
wanted a large society wedding. Besides, as Katherine
pointed out to Scott, it was her second marriage, and a
large formal wedding seemed inappropriate. Scott had
questioned her carefully, wanting to satisfy himself that she
was not just saying that because she knew all the publicity
would make him uncomfortable. She finally convinced him
that she did not want to be married on the society pages of
the newspaper any more than he did.

They had decided on a small private ceremony on Valentine's Day. The house Scott was having built would be
ready by then. Both had immediately fallen in love with the
large lot in Mill Valley. It was in a quiet neighborhood of
stately old oak trees. Scott had commissioned George
Weddington to design the house and had started a construction crew working on it as soon as the plans were
ready.

"Do you, Scott Justin Blake, take this woman...?" Even
though they had agreed on a small intimate ceremony, neither had ever dreamed they would actually end up getting
married on the spur of the moment on New Year's Eve
while dressed in ski clothes. But, as Scott had said, he could
not wait any longer. After getting over her surprise, Katherine had agreed. And now, here they were, standing in
front of a minister, exchanging their wedding vows.

Katherine lay in Scott's arms, nestled in the warmth of
the king-size bed. He slowly and sensually stroked his fingertips along the length of her body. "This is it, the wed-

ding night." He fixed her with a teasing grin. "Tell me, Mrs. Blake, are you prepared?"

She returned his teasing. "I think I'll be okay as long as you promise to be gentle with me."

He rolled her over on top of him and whispered in her ear, "I don't know, you get me so excited sometimes I lose all control." His hand slid seductively across the smooth roundness of her bare bottom.

She felt his growing arousal pressing against her. In a voice rapidly becoming thick with passion, she murmured in his ear, "I guess I'll just have to take my chances."

Her mouth found his as they melted into the heat of their passions, fueled by their deep and intense love for each other. Their tongues twined, their hands caressed and explored—their bodies became one. They made love with all the passion, yet all the tenderness, that each was capable of giving. Nothing existed at that moment beyond the deep and unconditional love they felt for each other.

The aroma of freshly brewed coffee slowly penetrated Katherine's sleep-fogged brain. She opened her eyes and reached across the bed for Scott. He was not there. She was about to get out of bed when he came through the door carrying a breakfast tray.

He smiled when he saw she was awake. "Good morning, sleepyhead. I was beginning to think you were going to spend the rest of your life in bed."

She grinned impishly at him. "I can think of far worse ways to spend the rest of my life." Her expression turned serious. "In fact, as long as you're with me I can't think of a better way to spend the rest of my life."

Scott set the tray on the nightstand, then sat down next to her. "I can't think of anything I'd rather do. I love you, Mrs. Blake."

She reached out and caressed his cheek. "I love you, too, Mr. Blake."

"It's a beautiful day. The sun is shining, the snow is sparkling and the air is crisp and clean. It's the first day of the year and—" he leaned forward and kissed her tenderly on the lips "—the first day of the rest of our lives together."

Epilogue

―――――

It was a warm summer morning, the first of July. Scott carried a breakfast tray into the bedroom and set it in front of Katherine. "Happy six-month anniversary." He leaned forward and kissed her.

"Mommy...Mommy..." Jenny burst into the room. Scott caught her just in time to avoid the disaster of her knocking over the tray and spilling the coffee all over the bed. "Look what Skippy did to my doll."

The little beagle puppy scampered into the room and tried to jump up on the bed. "No, you don't." Scott picked up the puppy, scratched him affectionately behind his long floppy ears, then placed him on the floor. "Not on the bed."

Jenny held the doll up to Scott. "Can you fix her, Daddy? Please, Daddy?"

He took the doll and the arm that the puppy had chewed off. "Let's look at it and see what we can do." After a closer inspection he realized that the doll's arm had actually been torn out of the socket rather than chewed in two. It could be repaired. "You know you can't leave your toys on the floor. Skippy is still a little puppy and he likes to chew on things." He went over to the French doors leading to the terrace and opened them, letting in the fresh air. "Why don't you and Skippy go play in the yard?"

"Come on, Skippy," Jenny called to the puppy as she ran outside, the puppy scampering after her.

"Look at her, Scott. Isn't it wonderful? She's finally able to be a happy little girl—a backyard with a swing and a little puppy to tag along after her. It's just the way I dreamed it would be. She hasn't had a single nightmare in months. It's almost as if they ceased the moment the ink was dry on the adoption papers."

"I was beginning to think we'd never get through all the red tape. I had no idea adoption was such a lengthy process. We started all this the first of November and it was the first of February before everything was finalized." He sat down on the bed next to her, enfolding her in his warm embrace. "I thought adoption was supposed to be quick—instant family as opposed to the good old-fashioned way." He tickled his fingers across her abdomen and kissed her cheek. "This little fellow—"

"Hold on, there. It was only yesterday that the doctor confirmed I was even pregnant. We don't know that it's going to be a boy. Maybe it will be a little girl."

"It has to be a boy—" he shot her mischievous grin "—otherwise I'll be badly outnumbered. The only man in a house full of women."

Katherine tried to give him a stern, serious look. "Don't be ridiculous. Skippy is a male."

He held her in his arms and brushed his lips lightly against her cheek as they watched Jenny and the puppy playing in the yard. "What kind of a name is Skippy for a dog? When he grows up all the other dogs will tease him."

"You know it's the only name Jenny wanted, from the moment she laid eyes on him."

Scott sighed as he repeated Katherine's words, more to himself than anyone else. "'Skippy is a male.' It's not quite the same, my love. It's not quite the same thing."

* * * * *

SILHOUETTE® *Desire*®

MYSTERY MATES!

Six sexy Bachelors explosively pair with six sultry Bachelorettes to find the Valentine's surprise of a lifetime.

Get to know the mysterious men who breeze into the lives of these unsuspecting women. Slowly uncover—as the heroines themselves must do—the missing pieces of the puzzle that add up to hot, *hot* heroes! You begin by knowing nothing about these enigmatic men, but soon you'll know *everything*....

Heat up your winter with:

#763 **THE COWBOY** by Cait London

#764 **THE STRANGER** by Ryanne Corey

#765 **THE RESCUER** by Peggy Moreland

#766 **THE WANDERER** by Beverly Barton

#767 **THE COP** by Karen Leabo

#768 **THE BACHELOR** by Raye Morgan

Mystery Mates—coming in February from Silhouette Desire. Because you never know who you'll meet....

HE'S MORE THAN A MAN, HE'S ONE OF OUR

Fabulous Fathers

EMMETT
Diana Palmer

What a way to start the new year! Not only is Diana Palmer's EMMETT the first of our new series, FABULOUS FATHERS, but it's her 10th LONG, TALL TEXANS and her 50th book for Silhouette!

Emmett Deverell was at the end of his lasso. His three children had become uncontrollable! The long, tall Texan knew they needed a mother's influence, and the only female offering was Melody Cartman. Emmett would rather be tied to a cactus than deal with that prickly woman. But Melody proved to be softer than he'd ever imagined....

Don't miss Diana Palmer's EMMETT, available in January.

Fall in love with our FABULOUS FATHERS—and join the Silhouette Romance family!

Silhouette
ROMANCE™

FF193

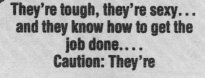

Take 4 bestselling love stories FREE
Plus get a FREE surprise gift!

For all those readers who've been looking for something a little bit different, a little bit spooky, let Silhouette Books take you on a journey to the dark side of love with

If you like your romance mixed with a hint of danger, a taste of something eerie and wild, you'll love Shadows. This new line will send a shiver down your spine and make your heart beat faster. It's full of romance and more—and some of your favorite authors will be featured right from the start. Look for our four launch titles wherever books are sold, because you won't want to miss a single one.

THE LAST CAVALIER—Heather Graham Pozzessere
WHO IS DEBORAH?—Elise Title
STRANGER IN THE MIST—Lee Karr
SWAMP SECRETS—Carla Cassidy

After that, look for two books every month, and prepare to tremble with fear—and passion.

SILHOUETTE SHADOWS, coming your way in March.

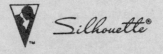

SHAD1